CONVERGENCE

SCOTT GULYAS

CONVERGENCE. Copyright © 2017 by Scott Gulyas.

ISBN 978-0-9993186-0-7
ISBN 978-0-9993186-1-4 (Ebook)

Library of Congress Control Number: 2017912982

Printed and bound in the USA
First Printing 2017

Published by Buckeye Publishing

This book is dedicated to my wife Laura and my family - thanks for supporting my crazy idea to write a novel!

And to my friend Rudy...I finally found something better to do.

PROLOGUE

From Wikipedia and everyday life experiences…

- Convergence:
  - The coming together of two or more separate, seemingly unrelated, factors or phenomenon resulting in sometimes unexpected consequences.

- Weather:
  - The state of the air and atmosphere at a particular time and place.
  - To deal with or experience something dangerous or unpleasant.

- Convergence Zone:
  - A region in the atmosphere where two prevailing flows meet and interact, usually resulting in distinctive weather conditions.

CONVERGENCE

CHAPTER 1

Thank God for the rain.

It started falling in big drops that evening. You know, those drops that when they hit the dry ground make a loud slapping noise. Ham could still hear the sound and smell the odd odor the rain brought with it those first few hours that Tuesday in October.

He'd always loved the rain. He had fond memories of playing outside in it as a young boy, umbrella be damned. The damp, musty smell as the first drops wet the ground. But falling with the drops this time was something else, something mixed in, something too small to be seen by the naked eye.

...something *best* to stay away from.

CHAPTER 2

Bad luck. Strange weather. Who's to say why things turn out the way they do. The prevailing easterlies might have spared many, thousands most likely, but the wind direction wasn't on the good people of Danville's side this day.

On this particular fall Saturday there was a unique convergence of a high pressure system coming out of the north, barreling straight down from Canada, and a stronger than expected low pressure front coming from the southwest. The two systems collided creating a convergence zone, as reported by Channel 7 weatherman Todd Prichard, stalling both systems over Danville, Ohio, for those fateful 12 hours. Convergence zone. It was the first time Todd had an opportunity to use that meteorological term since starting at Channel 7 three years ago. Todd burned five minutes of airtime explaining the technicalities of the unique weather phenomenon. He would have gone longer had it not been for the news director giving him the hand slicing across the throat motion from off set – the universal sign to cut it off now.

It seems like a little thing, inconsequential in the grand scheme of the national weather chart. That simple stall of stale air resulted in a 99.9% kill ratio in Danville. No convergence zone stall and the cloud would have quickly blown east. Passing over the largely unpopulated portion of Danville and Franklin County, exterminating a few unwanted rats and possums at the Tri-County Glosser dump, and harmlessly dissipated.

Bad luck?

Strange weather?

Might have…would have.

That's life.

Or maybe God really was napping that day in Danville…and the Devil was chuckling.

CHAPTER 3

Twenty-three years in public office. Who would have thought he'd last that long when he first entertained the idea of running for town treasurer. He didn't know much about being the town treasurer, actually nothing at all. What prompted him to run was that he'd heard that town officials had the inside track to the LLF licenses - LLF stood for Lake Limited Fishing licenses. Each year the state issued a small number of the LLF licenses. These highly sought after licenses allowed you to fish in the most pristine state lakes, but the state limited the number issued to avoid over-fishing these prime spots. And he had just bought himself a top of the line Bayliner bass fishing boat.

So that fall Nick Hammond ran for town treasurer and won. This was largely due to no one else opposing him - town treasurer was not one of the most glamorous city positions. Also aiding his victory was that the incumbent treasurer, Mildred Pearce (and yes…Mildred lived up to her name both in appearance, values, and ethics) was retiring at the ripe old age of 87. And of course his being famous in town as one of the Three just about guaranteed him winning the position.

So Nick Hammond, or Ham as his close buddies wanting connections to those LLF licenses called him, was sworn in as Danville town treasurer.

Ham was on the job all of 37 days when Dennis May, the popular and charismatic Danville mayor in his newly sworn in second term, was killed. Dennis, along with his pretty (Ham had always been attracted to her) wife Cindy, their 3 year-old daughter Katie, and their always well groomed poodle Harvey, were killed in a traffic accident. The dog dying always seemed like a positive to him since he was not a poodle lover. Give him a nice square block headed Lab or Golden Retriever any day of the week - sorry Harvey - no big loss there. But he hated to even think about little Katie in that accident, what a fucking waste of a beautiful life. Hello God…where were you he thought.

Hello God, where were you? He was saying and thinking that a hell of a lot these days.

Dennis and his family had been driving home on FM240, coming home from dinner out at their favorite Danville restaurant, Lucille's. The restaurant's Family Feast special was an all-you-can-eat Saturday night offer from 5-8 p.m. They were on their way back home when their Toyota Camry was hit head on by a drunk driver. The drunk driver was coming off a stop at the Third Base Tavern in his F-250 pickup. "Last Stop Before Home" was the tavern's motto, playing off the baseball theme. It was proudly displayed on their sign out front. A motto, Ham imagined, not fully endorsed by the Mothers Against Drunk Driving movement.

So Ham was asked to step into the open mayor position by the Danville town council and here he was twenty-three years later.

Of course if he had been in town the day of the accident instead of out fishing on his new boat at Lake Skinner...or if he had gone to his normal fishing spot on the east side of town, things would have been much different.

Most likely not town treasurer.

Most likely not mayor.

Most likely dead.

CONVERGENCE

If.

If.

He'd come to realize that was life…a series of seemingly unconnected events all coming together, building up momentum, and then….

God napping…Devil chuckling and all that bullshit.

CHAPTER 4

John's mind drifted as he drove. He thought about his life so far - John Tyler, age 31, born and raised in Danville, Ohio. He'd graduated from Danville High School with decent grades, but not National Honor Society material. He'd been the star center on the Danville Wildcats basketball team, but not star enough material to think about getting any college schola....

"What the hell!" he shouted out. His focus and thoughts came back to the road as he hit the brakes hard. A blue Honda Accord had just cut over in front of him, nearly taking off his front bumper as he inched forward along the on-ramp to the freeway.

On-ramp...freeway.

How things had changed, traffic at 5:23 a.m. in the morning...unfrickenbelievable! He thought back to high school, how he and his buddies used to make fun of this rinky-dink town. He remembers joking how it only had one traffic light...what had been a bit of an exaggeration - it had four. Making fun of all the old cronies that thought Danville had hit the big time since they had a McDonalds and then the final cherry on top...Walmart moved in.

This was *all* before Cardiff Technologies. Before they had *really, truly,* hit the big time.

As he inched along at three miles per hour, he looked around at the other drivers in this pre-dawn hour. Most stared straight ahead, looking almost like stuffed mannequins in their cars. Their hands frozen to their steering wheels at 10 and 2, just like they were taught so many years ago in their high school driver's education class. Several looked busy on their cell phones...texting, emailing, or making calls. Damned idiots! He had just read last week in the Danville Times about a little girl killed by a driver who had supposedly looked down at his phone to answer a text. He had run her over, right in front of her fucking house! A 6000-pound plus F-150 versus a 43-pound five year-old girl, it hadn't been much of a match up. It made him sick to his stomach to even think about it. Distracted driving was what the newspapers and law enforcement officials called it - he called it distracted living.

Most of them looked like zombies...half asleep. Going through the daily commute grinder. Just another day...the same as every other day. Thinking about the upcoming weekend. Thinking about lost dreams. Disillusioned. Just plain lost.

He threw himself into this last group – just plain lost. From the top of the world to just plain lost. The fall had been rapid and dramatic. He pounded down hard with both fists on the steering wheel. "What the hell went wrong!" he screamed to himself inside the car. Of course he knew very well the answer.

The drivers around him paid no attention. They rolled along beside him on their way to work, thinking of all the things on their daily to-do list, their windows rolled up, safe within their cars.

Oblivious to the horrors that lay ahead...

CHAPTER 5

John could still remember that first sneeze. That *damn* sneeze is what prompted Mary J to make the discovery. If only they'd left her behind that Saturday morning. They probably would have kept right on going down branch one, past that small opening, past where she found it.

Things could have been...*would* have been so different. After graduating from high school they probably would have lived out normal, Midwestern, boring lives in Danville. They probably would have worked jobs at the supermarket, hardware store, or the grain and feed store, and taken summer vacations down to South Carolina or maybe even Florida. They probably would have married, had a few kids, and been happy watching NFL football games on Sundays. Tossing back Rolling Rocks or

Pabst Blue Ribbons on weekends, sitting around complaining about the local economy, their bosses, Washington, D.C., and whoever the President was at the time. All the shit people do and spend their time complaining about in their normal lives.

What he wouldn't give to trade places with that life now...but it was too late. They'd all gotten exactly what they had dreamed about, what they *thought* they had always wanted – money, money, and more money. Even a little bit of fame had been mixed in – *their* 15 minutes in the spotlight.

Of course a lot of fucking good the money and fame had turned out to be – gone...*alllllll* fucking gone now.

CHAPTER 6

XR9-1...-2.

That single, incredibly simple, change in a number sequence haunted Ham. It seemed like he dreamt about it every night but it was hard to say, there had just been too many bad dreams all mixed together. The nightmares started soon after the accident. He would more often than not wake up in the middle of the night, his pillow soaked through with sweat, his heart racing as he relived the events from that October. It seemed all tangled together now. He closed his eyes, shaking his head...trying to clear it from his mind. But it didn't work - it was just too damn tangled.

The faces...the names on the lists...the goddamned smell. The smell would never leave him, it didn't matter how much time passed. He'd read somewhere how your sense of smell was the most powerful of the five senses and how a distinct smell could be burned into your memory for life. Those smart scientists got one right for once. He remembered right afterward how he'd tried to sneeze it out, even wash it out, but none of it worked. He eventually went to an ear, nose, and throat specialist to have his sinuses looked at. The doctor gave him a clean bill of health and told him it was "All in his mind." That may well be Ham thought…if only he could erase it all from his memory – the nightmares, the smell…most of all the names on the lists.

The XR9-1 strain aggressively attacked the human cellular structure from the inside out. It was unlike anything the Cardiff bioengineering team had ever seen, heard, or read about in any research and development study. It made Ebola look tame in comparison.

But Cardiff did not destroy the XR9-1 strain…they just shelved it. The final report from the bioengineering team simply stated "Requires further research". The electronic report was stored on the R&D department's secure military applications drive in a subfolder simply named XR9-1.

CHAPTER 7

John started at Cardiff as a lab technician, really not too bad for only having a high school diploma and two years experience at the Danville grocery store. He had actually rounded up his grocery store time to two years on the Cardiff employment application, in truth he had worked for 16 months as a bag boy. Not exactly a high tech skill set. Of course what really got his foot in the door was by being one of the Three. He smiled, which was rare for him these days. Funny, he thought...be in a cave at the right time, or wrong time he felt more and more so lately, and you too might have a chance to magically own a little piece of the world in Danville, Ohio.

He changed the radio station in his F-250 just as the mattress salesman was telling him about how well he would sleep on the latest and greatest Serta sleeper. It wasn't his damn mattress keeping him up at night. He hit preset two on the radio knowing that was Danville's FM98.7 WOLD. "Playing Only The Classics" was WOLD's motto, his go-to station for music. The Cure had just started singing "Disintegration," one of his favorites. He sang along with the lyrics like he'd done a hundred times before, his voice echoing the words of Robert Smith. But this time the words seemed to hold a different meaning for him...a *darker* meaning. It was if they were singing about his life.

The short-lived smile quickly faded from John's face.

CONVERGENCE

CHAPTER 8

Mary J stopped as she passed by the new small opening in the cave wall to her right. John and Ham were now well ahead of her, their headlamp lights reflecting off the walls of the narrow passageway. They paused for a moment discussing something...they were too far ahead for her to hear exactly what they were talking about. She heard John say something about not being able to see much and guessed he was referring to this new small hole in the cave wall. Then they split up, each going down different branches of the cave.

She sneezed, once...twice. They were those big kind of sneezes that just about lift your off your feet.

"Wow! You ok back there?" laughed John, as Mary J's sneezes echoed through the cave.

17

"Phew...yeah, I'm fine. Those were some doozies!"

Something in this area of the cave was triggering her allergies. She wiped at her itchy nose and re-adjusted the headlamp that had been jarred loose from the sneezes. She returned her focus to the cave wall and this new feature. Using her hands she felt around the new opening to make sure there weren't any sharp edges. It looked just big enough for her to poke her head through for a better look. Slowly...she eased her head through the opening in the wall. She was mindful not to knock the light off her forehead. The headlamps had been a great idea, the three of them had turned in their flashlights and bought the head mounted lights from the local camping store soon after discovering the cave. The headlamps allowed them to use their hands as they scrambled through the tight cavern spaces. With her head safely through the opening, she slowly rotated her headlamp beam, bathing the inside of the new opening with light. A shimmer from something on the wall caught her attention.

CHAPTER 9

Danville, Ohio, was not that different from a hundred other small towns in the Midwest. Historical documents state that the area was first settled in the late 1780s by a small group of American pioneers, descendants of the first Puritan English colonists that had settled New England. The pioneer families worked the fertile farmlands and lived in relative peace with the indigenous Iroquois Indians who called southern Ohio home, along with the Delaware, Shawnee, and Algonquin tribes.

Somewhere around 1815, the historical documents are not precise about the year, the relationship between these early settlers and the Iroquois turned sour. By all documented accounts, most of the men were killed off in battles with the Iroquois over farming land rights. It appears the remaining family members had died during ensuing battles between the Iroquois and Algonquin Indian tribes - the Algonquin's were expanding west during this time period, infringing on the Iroquois hunting grounds. The pioneer family member's deaths appear to be more attributed to collateral damage from these warring tribes versus from direct confrontation with the Indians. Death documents from the era are cloudy at best.

The now Danville area of the Ohio valley was essentially reclaimed by these two warring Indian tribes and remained that way for the next 30-plus years until somewhere around 1850. This is about the time that William Dan and his newlywed wife Evelyn settled in the area. This was not by her choice, but instead a result of a gambling win by her new husband William. His visit to a gambling parlor in late 1849 had paid off richly, a Jacks-over-7s full house won him a little over 1500 acres of Ohio farmland.

William Dan had been a printer by trade, the trade skill and small print shop passed down to him from his late father. He'd been named after his father but had never particularly liked the junior suffix, it always made him feel like a little kid, and so he dropped it once he came of age. The only mention of it was on his formal birth certificate. The print shop was located in Columbus, Ohio, and provided a very modest income for William and his wife Evelyn, enough for them to afford a small house on an average Columbus plot of land.

Upon winning the farmland William had some soul searching to do...he also had quite a bit of work ahead of him convincing Evelyn that they should try out the farming life on the newly won homestead. He did have a fallback plan - if all else failed he could always return to Columbus and re-open the print shop. So three months to the day after his winning hand, William and Evelyn packed up their three rooms worth of belongings onto their wagon and headed southeast out of Columbus.

It was a long and arduous journey over mostly undeveloped land in those days. They finally reached the nondescript acreage near midnight on the fourth day...and non-descript it was, much to her dismay only scrub brush and dirt as far as Evelyn could see by the light of the full moon.

Evelyn probably would have disagreed, but for William those first five years went by in a flash. They stayed busy putting in a well, constructing a small cabin, and planting an initial field of corn and beans. William did his homework reading up on farming techniques as well as what the most suitable crops were for the Midwestern soil and climate.

The nearby tribe of Iroquois Indians for the most part left them alone, too concerned with the ever-encroaching Algonquian tribes. The Algonquians posed a much greater threat than one crazy white man and his wife. William was actually able to befriend a few Iroquois from the nearby tribe who helped him with that first year's planting. They taught him the farming methods long used by the Iroquois people for planting, fertilizing, and harvesting the new crops.

Then in 1863 the transcontinental railway line started construction. It slowly snaked its way across the United States, connecting the West Coast with the existing Eastern United States rail network. A real estate broker acquaintance of William's, who was familiar with his gambling win five years prior, contacted William to inform him that the proposed rail line would be running very close to his existing acreage. The initial rail plans showed it running just a half-mile to the south of his property.

Acting on this information, William immediately bought up the adjoining, seemingly worthless 500 acres of land. Upon closing the deal, the happy seller reportedly told William "Enjoy the 500 acres of dirt!" shaking his head as he left, befuddled as to why anyone would want the worthless land and just happy to be finally rid of it. The 500 acres was just enough to bridge the gap between his property and the proposed rail line route. And as they say, the rest is history. The rail line did indeed come through, and very soon afterward the William Dan Feed Depot was established.

The Depot was the central supply hub to towns east and west for corn, grain, and cattle feed. The Dan family fortunes grew in lock step with the Depot business. A small community eventually sprouted around the Dan Feed Depot, the store providing much needed employment during those early hard economic years.

The new rail system also brought with it paying tourist passengers, and a surprising number of them liked what they saw and decided to stay. The community continued to grow and prosper. A church was built in 1867, which was used for both worship services as well as community meetings. The following year the community chose their first leader, William Dan. Then by unanimous vote in 1870, the community decided upon the name of Danville. Neither of which was surprising since William Dan's Feed Depot employed and fed most of the local population.

William became the first official Danville, Ohio, mayor in 1871, and held the post for the next 16 years. He died of tuberculosis in 1890, three years after stepping down as mayor. Evelyn followed him two years later from natural causes. During William's mayoral time, Danville quadrupled in size to 393 souls.

CHAPTER 10

Mary, or Mary J as all her friends called her at Danville High, was short for Mary Johnson. She never considered herself that pretty, at least not compared to the other popular cheerleader-type looking girls at Danville High. For one thing, she had too many freckles on her face for her liking. Also, her brown...almost auburn, hair never quite behaved like it should. She would spend hours in front of the bathroom mirror trying to style it like those fashion models she saw on the covers of Vogue or Cosmopolitan magazine that lined the grocery store checkout aisle. She would typically just give up and pull it back into a ponytail.

Of course that was her point of view. From the Danville High boy's perspective she was seen as pretty and easily approachable, much more so than those cheerleader-types she compared herself against.

She'd only been invited to come along by Ham a few days earlier. They had been sitting at the lunch table when he asked if she would be interested in joining John and him on a "little adventure exploring a possible cave" out behind their houses. She had a bit, quite a bit in truth, of a crush on Ham since her sophomore year so when he asked, she blurted out "Yes!" before really thinking about what "exploring a possible cave" might really mean.

There was no turning back now as the three slid down into the cavern opening.

CHAPTER 11

Ham and John had discovered what looked to be a cave opening the day before by chance, running across it during one of their post-school outings in the woods.

In their younger days the two would spend almost every spare moment they had trouncing around the woods. They'd start just after school and not return home until after dusk, sometimes much later. It was more than a few times that they'd both caught hell for coming home well after nightfall. When they did happen to stay out past dusk, Ham might receive a grounding for a few days from his parents, John on the other hand sometimes caught a slap alongside the head...or worse. John's father had a bad temper and a short fuse, not a good combination for his best friend. John's father had lost his job four years earlier due to Monsanto moving their Danville distribution center to their centralized plant in Columbus. Since that time he had acquired a new habit - drinking. Wild Turkey, straight up with three ice cubes was his style. *Three*...John remembers the time his mom made the first of the evening's drink with two. A few hard slaps later that blackened her left eye, and she had been taught a valuable lesson to not repeat that error. You throw in coming home late after exploring the woods with Ham...or as his dad would say "Fuck'n around in the woods!" and it was *guaranteed* to be a rough night. On those special occasions, John would sometimes come to school the next day with bruises on his arms and face. The school district had brought his dad in for several parent conferences, asking about the bruises, but this really only seemed to make matters worse. He'd sometimes wear long sleeve shirts to cover his arms, but there was no hiding his face - it always told the story. So needless to say, John did not shed any tears when his dad passed away from a combination of liver disease and stage IV lung cancer.

They had been wandering that day about the northeast portion of the woods, towards the edge closest to Hoover Dam. Ham had brought along two beers he'd lifted from his father's basement mini-fridge. He hoped his dad wouldn't notice it was light a couple this coming weekend, and even if he did the most he might expect to receive would be a few stern words. Doubtful even a grounding, Ham thought it worth the risk.

After close to an hour of hiking, the two decided they were far enough in to enjoy the beers without fear of being seen. It was as they surveyed the area for a fallen tree or rock outcrop to sit on, that Ham happened to notice something peculiar looking on the ground. What turned out to be the cave opening.

"What the hell's that?" Ham said pointing out the strange looking area just in front of where John was standing.

At first Ham just thought he was looking at a shadowed area from a ground overhang. Ground overhangs were something they'd run across many times before in other areas of the woods. They appeared where tree roots pushed the soft floor of the woods upwards, around large hidden rocks or other tree roots. If the ground eventually pushed up far enough, it would fold over on itself creating an overhang. Squatting down to get a better look, Ham quickly realized there was a hole or opening in the ground further back under the overhang. John had joined him, kneeling down next to Ham to see for himself.

"Cool," they both said in unison. Then quickly followed it up with a "Jinx – you owe me a Coke!" and then both broke out in laughter.

After a few more minutes discussing their find, they quickly came to the conclusion that they'd need more light to get a better view under the dark ground swell. And since neither one had brought along a flashlight they thought it best to stop for the day. Pulling up next to each other on a nearby fallen tree, they sat and drank the now lukewarm beers. They talked about how it might be a cave...an exciting prospect...but that it was more likely just a beginning of a sinkhole - sinks were quite common around these parts of the Ohio Valley. They finished their beers in silence, enjoying the peacefulness of the woods. Stashing the empty cans next to the overhang, they took one last look into the dark opening and hurried home. Neither wanted to be late tonight and risk their parents not allowing them to come back out the next day to properly check out their new discovery.

29

CHAPTER 12

The three took turns sliding on their stomachs under the overhang and squeezing through the narrow opening in the ground. A cool draft of musty smelling air was flowing out of the cave entrance, washing over them as they slipped through the opening. It smelled of damp wood and leaves. The narrow cave opening had been camouflaged by the slight lip of the overhang, almost covering the opening completely.

One by one they slid under the lip and then dropped into the cave. First in was John. He held his small pocket flashlight in his mouth as he maneuvered his body through the opening and then suddenly disappeared from sight. A few seconds later a loud "Whoop!" came up from the darkness beneath the overhang. From their kneeling positions looking beneath the overhang lip, Ham and Mary J could now see John's flashlight beam now dancing wildly around from inside the opening.

"Uh...you ok down there?" Ham yelled back.

"C'mon you guys, it's cool down here!" John replied. "But be careful as you drop down, there's tons of roots sticking out...especially right at the beginning."

Mary J was the second one down. She stuffed her flashlight into her jean's pocket and started inching her way under the overhang lip feet first.

"Good luck!" Ham joked, smiling at her as she slowly slid out of sight.

John saw her right leg swing into the cave's mouth, temporarily blocking the small sliver of daylight streaming in from the outside world. He repositioned his flashlight back in his mouth, freeing up his hands to help Mary J down. As she dropped in, John guided her legs around the roots sticking out at all angles from the wood's floor.

"Phew – thanks for the help!" Mary J said excitedly as she dropped down the last foot and balanced herself on the uneven cave floor next to John.

She didn't know John all that well from school, but it still gave her some sense of security to be standing side-by-side with him here in the darkness. Mary J dug her flashlight out of her pocket and switched it on, the small light beam providing her a little relief from the darkness of the cave. John and Mary J's flashlights illuminated the interior of the small cavern room in which they stood. She looked at herself standing there in the cave entrance, looking up at a sliver of light through a tangle of tree roots...she was *truly* beginning to question that "Yes" response she was so quick to offer when asked by Ham at lunch. This adventure exploring the woods wasn't quite what she'd imagined.

"Everything ok down there?" Ham yelled from above. He was trying to peer down through the cave opening to see if it was clear for him to start crawling in.

"Yes! - Yes!" John and Mary J yelled back in unison.

"Jin...!" John caught himself mid-jinx unsure how Mary J might react.

John was one of those boys who had always considered Mary J very pretty and therefore had never gathered the courage to approach her to ask out on a date. Other than working alongside each other on a few in-class team assignments, they had only exchanged an occasional "How's it going" passing each other in the school hallways. It was also obvious to John that her eyes were always, and had always been, focused on Ham. Ham only finally realizing this at the start of the past school year. And why not in Mary's defense. Ham was just plain and simply damn likable. He wasn't the typical high school jock with all muscles and nothing behind it. John sometimes found himself jealous of Ham, but that feeling had always taken a backseat to their friendship. The two had been the best of friends for as long as he could remember. Thinking back now it must have been since fourth or fifth grade.

Ham's family had moved into John's neighborhood from Columbus, or maybe it was Cincinnati, he couldn't remember anymore. They had bought the house four down from John's. As fate would have it, they ended up seated next to each other in Mrs. Beagler's homeroom class and immediately hit it off. They were always in constant competition to be the class clown. Trying to one-up each other's antics and push Mrs. Beagler right up to the edge of her sanity, much to the delight of the rest of the class.

They continued to be inseparable outside of class. The wooded area behind their houses was their personal playground; it seemed to stretch on forever in the minds of the curious and exploring 8 year olds. Any free time they had was spent there - exploring, building tree houses, playing hide-and-seek, and more often than not just getting into trouble. Hiding out from the rest of the world. They'd barely even stop home after school to say "Hi!" and "Bye!" again to their moms before they were off running out to the woods.

The woods were part of the Central Ohio Valley Recreational area. The recreation area encompassed a total of 5330 acres. The area nearest Danville was heavily wooded with white and black ash, elms, and sugar maples. Eventually the heavy woods gave way to meadowland as you worked your way south from Danville. There were two main visitor entrances, the Kingsgate entrance on the eastern side and the Jamestown entrance on the northwestern side. Fishing was allowed in the two large ponds within the recreation area and there were numerous hiking and biking trails. The wooded area where Ham and John spent most of their time exploring was at the northeastern most tip of the recreation area. Here there were no established hiking or biking trails, so visitors were rare, making it feel like it was their own personal woods.

"Ok – I'm coming down!" shouted Ham as they heard him start to slide into the cave's mouth. As he dropped down he brought with him a mix of leaves, sticks, and dirt.

Ham weighed in at about 180 pounds while John tipped the scale at maybe 150 soaking wet. So needless to say, John wasn't quite as willing to help Ham down as he had been the much lighter...and much *cuter*, Mary J. John also didn't want to risk

Ham losing his balance and falling on him right in front of Mary J, *that* was not going to happen. He had made it down on his own and so could Ham.

John and Mary J watched as Ham's legs appeared in the opening above them, they both backed up against the cave wall to give him room below. He struggled a bit more than they had coming down due to his larger body frame, but finally wiggled through and dropped the last few feet. He hit the cave floor awkwardly, lost his balance, and ending up falling on his ass just on the other side of Mary J.

"*Nice*...very graceful big guy!" John took full advantage of the opportunity to poke some fun at Ham in front of Mary J. She followed up with a few giggles, which only widened the smile on John's face.

"What the hell bonehead, thanks for the help down!" Ham replied back to John as he stood and brushed off his jeans. Then he laughed too at his ungraceful entrance and landing. Along with his athletic build, good personality, and brains, Ham was never shy about laughing at himself for some of the stupid things he did.

Ham fished his flashlight from his pocket and switched it on, all three of their flashlight beams now bathing the small cavern room with light. The room was narrow and quite long – it probably wasn't more than five feet across at its widest point and close to

15-20 feet long. The ceiling slanted up from eight feet or so high, where the sliver of daylight was streaming in from the narrow slit opening to the woods directly above them, to maybe 12 feet at the opposite side.

The three stood motionless in the darkness, their eyesight and hearing slowly adjusting to the cave's environment. They could hear a steady babbling of water from maybe a small creek and a full orchestra of water drips echoing off the cave walls. It was hard to know if the noises were five feet in front of them or 100 yards off, the sounds playing tricks on their ears as it reflected off the cavern walls.

There were two narrow but passable crack openings, one was located directly under the cave lip where they stood, the other at the far end of the room. The one closest to them was filled with roots growing across its entrance, reflecting back the light from their flashlights. It would be rough going if they had to clear these out, and what lay beyond the root barrier was difficult to see. The crack on the opposite side looked to be clear and so without any discussion they naturally started moving in that direction.

CHAPTER 13

The 5330 acre recreation area that Ham and John called their backyard was shaped almost like a perfect rectangle with its east-west boundary approximately 130 acres long and its shorter north-south boundary a bit over 40 acres tall. While not as large as some of the wooded areas in the southern part of the state, to them it seemed endless. It was their personal Neverland.

The eastern edge of the recreation area butted up against Hoover Dam. The western corner crossed over from Franklin County into adjoining Taylor County, at which point Highway 14 crossed through it before the woods continued on for another mile.

The acreage was a mix of both county and state owned property that butted up against private landowners. Private property lines were not always clearly identified which was typical in this area of the country, so it was never quite clear exactly where you stood. Thus Ham and John always kidded each other about catching some buckshot, either from one of the private property owners unhappy about trespassers on their land or a hunter mistaking them for a deer in season.

The recreation area had not always been so rectangular shaped. A large percentage of the original wooded area in Franklin County was now covered by water backed up behind Hoover Dam.

The Army Corps of Engineers built the dam back in 1934 to control flooding of the Alum River, which sliced through the easternmost quarter of Franklin County. The dam also provided a reliable irrigation source for the then burgeoning farming community.

Prior to the dam's construction, the woods stretched south another 500 or so acres, ending just at the northern edge of Jefferson County.

The western-most portion of the woods had burned in the fire of 1951. That year, due to extreme drought and some careless teenager's campfire, the entire western half of Franklin County had burned. The fire was eventually contained as the wind unexpectedly shifted on the fourth day of the firefight. The Danville fire department, captained by Ted Neely, alongside firefighters from the neighboring Jefferson and Taylor counties held the fire line. And with the wind shifted in their favor, they were finally able to fully contain and extinguish the fire 10 days later.

Because of the '51 fire, about half of the current 5330 acre span was relatively new growth. The original, or old growth, wooded area that avoided the fire was much more densely covered with the mature hardwood trees, but with additional scrub brush, thorny undergrowth and briar patches.

The cave entrance was located in this old growth area. It was probably the inhospitable thorny undergrowth and briars that allowed the entrance to remain undiscovered for so many years. Most day visitors and hikers that came to the recreation area woods stayed on the trails in the new growth areas. And for good reason, hiking in these areas did not mean pulling thorns and cat's claw briars from your boots, jeans and lower legs for an hour after a hike.

If the fire of '51 had burned another 500 yards east, and if the cave entrance had been discovered by one of the firefighters, it probably would have been filled in. They most likely would have done so as a safety precaution to ensure none of their firefighting brothers twisted an ankle or broke a by leg inadvertently stepping into the cave's entrance.

If.

SCOTT GULYAS

If.

Probably would have been.

More of that God napping and Devil chuckling thing.

CHAPTER 14

Ham led the way through the narrow crack opening at the far end of the cavern room. Mary J followed closely behind Ham with John bringing up the rear in a single file line.

"You ok?" John asked Mary J.

"Yeah – I'm fine" she replied trying to sound confident and hoping neither Ham nor John heard the slight waver in her voice.

Truth be told she was questioning herself. Questioning why the heck (she rarely cursed, even when talking to herself in her own head) she was down here in this dark, damp, cramped cave.

Yeah sure she wanted to hang out with Ham, whom she thought was a knockout...but was this worth it? Her friends had grown jealous since Ham had finally taken notice of her this past year. But now looking at herself standing there…there in this sliver of passageway, God knows how many feet underground, with just a few sweeping chaotic flashlight beams lighting their way and now talking about going forward…*deeper*…into the cave. Well, she was beginning to think this was not such a dandy idea after all, Ham or no Ham.

As she inched forward through the crack she felt John bump up against her shoulder.

"Sor…sorry," John stammered out.

John had always liked Mary J, even though he had probably said maybe 10 words total to her in high school. Now standing right next to her in the cramped cave passageway, smelling her perfume…he had been daydreaming, momentarily forgetting about their cramped confines, and had ended up walking right into her. Very smooth move he thought to himself.

Ham sidestepped his way through the crevice passageway. His 6'1" athletic frame, while serving him well on the football field, was not the optimum size to be caving through a narrow fissure. His back and chest rubbed up against both walls of the passageway, he barely fit.

The passageway sloped downward now, steeply in some areas, as they continued on for another 50 yards or so. The air seemed to drop a few degrees with each step they took down the slope.

John broke the silence around them with a yell.

"Look up there!" he shouted. His voice seemed twice as loud in the narrow confines of the cave's passageway.

The crevice they'd just passed through had been two feet wide at best, with the ceiling only a foot or two above their heads when they had first entered. Now as John looked up, he estimated it to be almost 20 feet or more to the ceiling.

The beams from their flashlights washed over the ceiling. The extra headroom made it seem like they had a bit more freedom in the cave, a little less claustrophobic feeling. They could see roots jutting out from the cracks in the ceiling as the trees far above them sent out their feelers looking for water sources below...only to break through the cave ceiling and end up still thirsty.

Spider webs dotted the walls and ceilings, Mary J shivered when she saw all the silvery webs. She was *not* a big fan of spiders, especially not while squeezing through a tight crevice in a dark cave with nowhere to run!

Mary J looked back towards Ham and realized he was now almost 20 feet in front of her. He was on the move again after quickly surveying the ceiling opening.

The separation from him here in the dark suddenly made her feel alone and exposed. She told herself to just relax and breathe - John was probably less than five feet behind her. She could hear his breathing but couldn't actually see him without turning her head, which wasn't easy in the cramped passageway. He was there...that was his breathing she heard...she was fine she told herself. Nonetheless, she gripped her flashlight a little tighter and quickly slid forward, intent to close the gap and catch up to Ham.

As they moved forward, the crevice passageway remained a tight fit but passable. Water sometimes dripped down the walls dampening their clothes and muddying the narrow pathway. John could feel his feet grow heavy as the mud began to cake to his Converse high tops. He knew his mom would be asking questions about what he had gotten himself into this time when she saw his shoes and dirty clothes that night.

John noticed that Ham and Mary J had stopped in the passageway. Their flashlight beams, side-by-side, were both pointing directly back at him. He slowly inched forward, having to squeeze through one last very tight rock outcropping. Pushing through, he emerged into an open room...what the group would eventually refer to as the pinch point room.

The room was roughly circular in shape, maybe 12 feet in diameter. It provided them a welcome respite from the confining crevice passageways they'd traveled through over the past hour.

"That's better," said Ham with a sigh of noted relief. "I was getting tired of that damn crack."

Each of them was brushing off their clothes the best they could from the dirt, mud, and spider webs they'd swept from the cave walls.

Mary J pounded her shoes on the ground trying to knock off some of the mudpacks. "My feet feel like they weigh 20 pounds!" she remarked with both Ham and John echoing the sentiment.

"Yuck," she exclaimed, as a large mud slab fell from her shoe.

"Yep...my mom is going to come unglued when she sees my clothes," said John.

"Oh crap!" Ham was pointing his flashlight up the wall, focusing on a hole almost 20 feet above them.

John and Mary J's flashlight beams swung over to combine with his. All three lights now illuminating the roughly three-foot hole cut right into the featureless rock wall face. The group silently surveyed the surrounding wall, all three coming to the same conclusion in their heads. The room had no other exits and the only way forward was through this small hole. No one spoke as they each let this sink in.

"I hate to say it," said John, "but I think we're done for today. It's getting late anyways and we're going to need a ladder and some rope to get up there if we want to go any further."

"Hell yes we want to go further!" Ham said quickly - just in case either of the other two was thinking of calling it quits after their first day of caving. "But I agree, we are stuck for now."

Mary J, having not said a word since they'd entered the room, felt a bit relieved that they had to turn back for now. She'd had more than enough for one day.

It took another hour and a half for the three to backtrack through the cave passageways to the entrance. After making their way out, they stood in the now twilight of the early spring night listening to the woods coming alive with noises from crickets, frogs, and cicadas. They switched off their flashlights, smiling at one another as they surveyed each other's dirty faces, clothes, and shoes.

"That was a lot of fun!" John said.

"Hell yes! And next time I'm definitely wearing some beater clothes!" said Ham laughing.

They traipsed back through the woods towards home talking about their first day in the cave, feeling exhausted and sore from contorting their bodies through the narrow passageways. Each with at least a few minor elbow cuts and knee scrapes, each excited about what may lay ahead of them.

CHAPTER 15

They had bought the headlamps the very next day at the camping equipment store downtown. Over the next five weeks they made numerous trips back into the cave, each time they explored a little farther along the cave's maze of passageways. They shuttled in a small ladder, rope, water, and some snacks to store in the pinch point room. The room aptly named by the three after the first time they'd squeezed through the small hole in the room's rock face.

The ladder had allowed them to reach the small hole - their initial estimate of its size had turned out to be generous. Once reached the hole turned out to be more rectangular than circular and it was at best two feet tall by three feet wide. This meant they had to wiggle through on their stomachs to gain entry. Using the rope, John rigged up a makeshift dumbwaiter, which allowed them to shuttle food and supplies up to the entrance of the hole. From the pinch point room the cave extended another 400 yards before branching off into at least a half dozen different directions.

One-by-one the group explored each of these new passageways. They discovered a number of smaller rooms along the way, but none the size of the pinch point room. John maintained a meticulous map of the cave. Each day he'd spend time scribbling down the passages they'd explored, what was found, and noting any dead ends. He also highlighted markers they'd left on the cave walls to be sure they found their way back out. Most of these new passages were very similar to those below the pinch point. Tight crevices filled with roots that ripped at their clothes, and the same thick mud that clung to their now ruined sneakers. The cave mud seemed to permanently stain their sneakers. No matter how hard they tried to wash or scrub it off the canvas fabric, their sneakers always ended up with a reddish tint.

They also continued to run across lots of spiders...the largest being, to Mary J's extreme displeasure, almost the size of her hand. The group had made spider finding into a game. It had been John's idea; he started keeping track of the largest ones they ran across. In case of a tie or disagreement, John was the official spider-referee, able to cast the deciding vote if they thought one was going to takeover the top spot.

They'd come across quite a few passageways they were not able to go down, the crevice walls sometimes almost closing upon themselves cutting off their path. Other times they'd come across forks where there were two passable routes, they would mark the unexplored route with a large O to let them know it was still an option to explore. Still other passageways they'd come across were either completely or partially blocked by rocks and roots that the group deemed impassable, or at a minimum just didn't look like much fun to try to clear out. So these were also abandoned as exploratory options.

Forward and deeper into the cave they explored. Some days they wouldn't go more than 50 yards further due to the rough going, other days they might cover 300+ yards. John's map continued to grow more impressive each day as he added to the cave's web of passageways.

It was towards the end of the fifth week that the group started to discuss the prospect that they may be nearing the end of the cave system. The main cave pathway seemed to be slowly narrowing in both width and height. All three needed to now hunch over most of the time as they continued deeper into the cave. Ham took on the most scrapes and bruises, determined to follow John and Mary J through even the tightest cracks and crevices.

That was before the rain.

Over the next three weeks Danville was inundated with twice its *yearly* rainfall total. Todd Prichard from Channel 7 was as surprised as the town's people at the amount of rain from the storm system. The weathercaster just kept repeating the old adage "April showers will bring May flowers" each night as he signed off. As the rain continued into the third week, he kept up with the sign off adage…but it was more of a whisper, and it was minus his typical broadcaster smile. *He* was beginning to wonder when the rain would stop. While the local Danville farmers were happy with the water for their crops, they were equally unhappy with the so-much-so-fast deluge that in turn washed away their valuable seed and fertilizer.

When the rain finally did stop at the end of that third week, it was another week before the group tried to re-enter the cave. Ham had gone out to check the cave's entrance right after the storm let up. When he shined his flashlight under the overhang all he could see was water, the cave was flooded. So it was four weeks and one day before the three finally re-entered on that early May afternoon.

John had replayed the timing in his head a hundred times…hell, maybe a thousand times, since that fateful day.

If Ham and he hadn't first stopped to enjoy those stolen beers in that exact spot.

If they had stopped at the pinch point and decided not to go on any further.

If it hadn't rained so damned much that April.

If they had just decided to go in alone that Saturday morning and left Mary J and her goddamned allergies behind.

If.

If.

If.

If.

If God wasn't napping.

CHAPTER 16

The water level at the cave opening had subsided a couple days before, but the three had decided over their lunchtime cafeteria pizza that it would probably be smart to give it until the weekend to dry up inside. This would also allow them to get an early start that Saturday morning since it now took almost two hours to reach their farthest point of exploration in the cave system. Another added benefit they all three hoped for was that by waiting the few extra days the cave wouldn't be a complete mud pit when they got down there. Their moms were getting tired of constantly running their sneakers through the washing machine.

So they decided to meet that next Saturday morning, 8 a.m. sharp at the cave.

John as usual was first to arrive. He was sitting on the same log where the two had first enjoyed those warm beers as Ham walked up around 8:15 a.m. John had got there an hour earlier, so excited about getting back down into the cave that he hadn't slept much the night before. He had toyed with the idea of going in solo, but had decided against it since he knew Ham and Mary J would give him the business if he went in without them.

"Did you see Mary J?" John asked Ham as he walked up and took a seat next to him on the log.

Ham hadn't and John was getting antsy about having to wait much longer. The two sat talking, both excited and a bit worried about what damage the rain may have done in the cave. They just hoped the cave passageways weren't completely blocked by the flood debris. Neither wanted to spend the day digging through sticks and mud, re-clearing the paths they'd already explored.

As 9 a.m. neared there was still no sign of Mary J. They were just about to start in without her when they heard someone coming through the woods.

"Hey guys wait up!" she yelled out once she spotted them. She had been running and was out of breath as she joined up.

"Sorry...I'm...late," she said between breaths, "my stupid allergies kept me up all night sneezing and I slept right through my alarm this morning." She stood rubbing her bloodshot eyes, her breathing slowly coming back to normal.

"No biggie, let's go," Ham replied.

Ham led the way back into the cave. As he slid through the entrance, he was shocked at how much debris was on the cave floor. It looked to be covered by a foot or more of leaves, branches, and rocks. He even saw a few wrappers from some of their snack supplies they'd stashed at the pinch point room. That wasn't a good sign. It was hard to imagine the water being able to push them through the labyrinth of cavern passageways to the entrance room. He was no longer very optimistic about how the rest of the cave would look after seeing this. The loose mix of fresh debris on the cave floor made the footing a bit tricky as Ham steadied himself and prepared to guide Mary J down.

"Careful coming down guys," Ham yelled back up topside, "there's a bunch of crap down here on the floor...I almost twisted my ankle when I landed!"

After Mary J and John were safely down, the three focused their headlamps down the main passage they'd traveled dozens of times over the past few months.

"Oooohhh shit!" Ham exclaimed as their headlamps illuminated the blocked passageway.

"What a mess!" agreed John.

Mary J was silent, finally whispering a "Yuck," as the three stood frozen in disbelief at what they were seeing.

What had always been a tight and narrow passageway was now a solid wall of tangled branches. The debris blockage was flush to the cave's ceiling. They worked the next two hours clearing the crevice. The going was slow as they shuttled the branches they removed back into the entrance room and piled them against one wall. After dismantling the initial blockage, the group was relieved to see the passageway beyond was relatively clear. They proceeded with little effort until reaching the pinch point room.

There they found the ladder all but covered under the debris flow on the floor. After digging it out they were happy to see that it had only suffered a few new dents on its aluminum frame. John propped it back up against the cave wall just under the pinch point hole opening. The ladder now stood at least a foot taller atop the debris flow on the floor.

"Well that's the first good thing to come out of this flood, " John said. The extra height would make it easier to reach and climb through the hole.

As they expected, the remainder of their supplies had been washed away. Probably buried beneath the debris in one of the cave's many side passageways. "Sacrifices to the cave Gods" they all agreed, trying to make the best of the situation.

One by one they scaled the ladder and squeezed through the pinch point hole. Once through, they proceeded down what the group referred to as the western hallway. The three foot wide by seven foot tall passageway was named by Ham who pointed out that it reminded him of walking down his hallway at home. The similar dimensions along with the fact the straight passageway ran due west by John's compass, and the name had stuck.

The hallway extended on for about 30 yards or so before finally branching off into four smaller crevices, these were more typical of what they were used to squeezing through. They had simply named them branch one, two, three, and four based on their size - number one being the largest, four being the smallest. Branches three and four had been explored until the passageways either reduced in size making them impassable or just abruptly dead-ended at a wall. These dead-ends occurred where the water that formed the cave system, eating its way through the soft limestone, finally met up against a harder rock formation and called it quits. Prior to the rain they'd been focusing their efforts exploring branches one and two.

"Look there," Ham was pointing his headlamp beam down the hallway at an oddly shaped dark spot located on the wall separating branches one and two. It looked like a new small opening that none of them remember having been there before the recent deluge.

Ham was first to reach the new opening. Upon closer inspection though he saw it was maybe only about 12 inches across, making it impossible for him to put his head through for a better look. He pointed his headlamp beam in but couldn't make out much detail of what lay inside.

"Bummer - it's too damn small to see anything inside," he called back to John and Mary J who were still making their way down the hallway corridor.

He scanned the section of the wall where the new hole was located. The rock around the hole was solid, he hit it a few times with the palm of his hand – no hollow sounds. There must have been a small section of softer limestone that finally gave way, yielding to the force of the recent water flowing through the cavern from the storm. After his brief stop to investigate, Ham readjusted his headlamp and started down branch one to see if there were any other new discoveries left behind by the floodwaters.

John was the next in line coming down the hallway. As he passed the new opening he glanced in, trying to angle his headlamp for a better view. There just wasn't enough of an opening to get a clear look inside the hole. John paused for a moment - he flashed his headlamp beam over branch one. He could see Ham maybe 10 yards down the passageway. He smiled to himself as he thought about how comfortable they'd gotten exploring the spider web of caverns by themselves. A big difference compared to those first few days when they rarely were separated from each other by more than a few feet. They now knew the various branches like the back of their hands and had grown accustomed to how their voices traveled in the cave, no longer freaked out by the echoes that initially were so disorientating. Making one last check on Ham, John redirected his headlamp beam and attention down branch two and walked on.

Mary J was only a few feet behind John. As she approached the new wall opening, she flashed her headlamp beam down branches one and two, taking visual inventory of Ham and John's location. Ham was almost out of view down branch one - she could just barely make out the emblem on the back of his Quicksilver t-shirt. John was only 10 feet or so down branch two.

She redirected her headlamp beam back at the small opening in the wall directly in front of her. She placed her hand up to the opening, there seemed to be a slight draft coming out of the hole. As she moved forward to peer into the opening, the draft wafted across her face. That's when she felt it...a slight tickle in her nose. Something was setting off her allergies. She sneezed, once...twice. "Ugh...I hate these allergies," she whispered to herself as she wiped at her nose. She repositioned her headlamp that had been jarred loose from the sneezes and returned her focus to this new small hole. Mary J had a distinct advantage over the boys, her smaller frame allowed her to fit her face and headlamp right up to the opening. She gazed into the hole, her headlamp beam illuminating the inside of the crevice. She looked inside briefly and then pulled her face away from the opening.

That was odd...had she seen a *glow*?

It happened so quickly that she wasn't quite sure if it had been there or not. Repositioning her face back up to the hole in the rock face, she closed her eyes tight, waiting for all the afterimages to fade from her vision. Mary J opened her eyes and then slowly moved her head back through the opening. She focused her attention on the inside walls of the hollow opening, to her amazement they were glowing! They couldn't be of course, she figured her eyes must have been playing tricks on her. The cave being absolutely pitch black and her headlamp having such a singular bright beam - her eyes must be struggling with the contrast. Focusing and refocusing as different things passed in and out of the lamp's beam. Yes that must be it, the contrast messing with her eyes.

Withdrawing her head, she slowly stepped back from the opening, her brain trying to make sense of what she just saw. Bioluminescence...the word sprang to her mind. She remembered learning about it in their Bio class with Mr. Samuelson.

She once again placed her head back through the small opening. This time trying not to move, she focused the beam from her headlamp on one localized area of the interior wall, then slowly reached up and switched off her headlamp. The walls inside were brilliantly lit with an eerie green glow. Both startled and excited, she quickly pulled her head from the small opening forgetting all about the tight fit. Her forehead scraped on the hole opening's exit, sending her headlamp tumbling to the ground. In the darkness she wiped at her smarting forehead, already damp with blood seeping from the scrape.

"Ahhh...hey guys!" she yelled, smiling to herself, "c'mon back here, I found something you'll *definitely* want to see!"

CHAPTER 17

The three spent the remainder of that Saturday afternoon chipping away at the small new opening. Using John's small pocketknife they were able to enlarge it enough by day's end for Ham and John to be able to peek into the new cavern room. The opening was just large enough now for them to witness the inside wall's bioluminescent reaction.

Enlarging the hole also allowed them a better view of the size of this new room. It was much larger than they had initially assumed, appearing to span the entire width between branches one and two. They guessed the walls were less than a foot thick to the outside branch one and two passageways, which was probably why the recent flooding was enough to break through a weak spot in the wall. The room also looked quite deep, but it was hard to say for sure from their limited viewpoint. It sloped steeply downward, the ceiling reflecting their headlamp beams at the far end of the room. While the new room size was impressive, it was the eerie glow that was the main topic of their conversation.

They didn't really start using the term "bioluminescence" until days later, after they had researched the phenomenon. In those first few days they simple referred to it as "the glow."

"It's weird...like the cave walls have some sort of coating or moss on them," Mary J observed. She was sweeping her headlamp beam back and forth across the walls and ceiling of the new room.

Ham reached through the hole stretching to touch the closest glowing portion of the side wall with his hand. He wiped his index finger across the rock face and withdrew his arm. Mary J and John stood next to him as he aimed his headlamp beam at the smear of greenish-brown goo on his finger.

"Switch off your lights," Ham told John and Mary J. They both reached up and toggled off their headlamps. Ham then turned his off and all three stood in complete darkness. They had all expected to see the same bright glow coming from his finger...but nothing, not even a glimmer.

"Hmm...that's strange," said Ham. He toggled back on his headlamp and pointed the beam directly at his finger for closer inspection. They huddled around Ham, nothing except the sound of drips coming from one of the far off passageways and their breathing could be heard in the cave. The cave temperature was just low enough so they could see each other's breath as it floated through their headlamp beams.

"Somehow you ruined it," John said breaking the silence. "Nice job idiot," he joked to Ham punching him in the shoulder.

"Maybe you squished whatever makes it glow when you wiped it with your finger," John said.

"Hey, have you guys ever seen the TV nature shows about those things that live in the ocean and at night when you splash around in the water the water glows?" asked Mary J. She had seen that on one of the shows her mom loved watching on cable TV. "Maybe this stuff is alive and you killed it when you smeared your finger through it."

On queue, John started whistling the tune from the X-Files. All three of them felt a little creeped out as they considered what Mary J had just said...the idea that this moss-like coating was alive.

"Very nice touch smart ass," replied Ham, returning the shoulder punch to John. "I've got an idea, let's scrape some off and have Mrs. M look at it."

Mrs. M was Mrs. Julie McMeekan, Danville High's science and chemistry teacher. Mrs. M was one of the student's favorite teachers. She had the rare ability to connect with the students both on an academic level, earning the kid's respect for her technical book knowledge, as well as on a social level. She was also one to never miss a chance at cracking a joke about the latest fashion or music trend the kids seemed to jump on.

"Great idea," agreed Mary J, "we can put some of it in here."

She pulled out a small plastic baggie from her jean pocket, it was full of multicolored candy Skittles. She had brought them along as a surprise snack for the three of them, and had planned on giving them out on their way back home. She emptied the candy into her hand and then portioned them out equally to Ham, John, and herself. They stood motionless for a few minutes in a circle, the beams from their headlamps focused on their open palms. The bright colors of the Skittles candies standing out in stark contrast to the pitch black of the cave surroundings. Each chewing on their Skittle allotment - each savoring the different flavors. Long after they'd finished they continued to dig the gummy candy residue from their teeth with their tongues.

"Man I love these things," Ham blurted out, "especially the grape ones."

"Ugh, grape is the *worst*," said John, "you're nuts, gotta go orange."

"Ok - you're both wrong," insisted Mary J, unable to stay out of this important conversation about her favorite snack candy. "Green is the best – I say go green or go home!" her shout echoing in the cave.

All three burst out in laughter. For a moment they forgot all about the cave and the strange eerie glowing moss. For a moment they were just high school teenagers enjoying Skittles.

***

How John remembered that moment, seemingly frozen in time in his mind…it seemed like a lifetime ago. It was one of those memories we all have where it's so damn real and clear in your memory, as they say, "Like it was yesterday." He could still smell the mustiness of the cave, feel the cool damp air, hear the distant water dripping as it seeped through the ground from above…and taste those delicious orange Skittles.

He smiled and licked his lips; he could *almost* taste a slight hint of orange.

CHAPTER 18

"Asshole!" John shouted out in his car as he was cut off merging onto the 425 freeway.

The 425 ran around the perimeter of Danville. The outer belt was completed 10 years ago as the city outgrew its central downtown confines and started spreading outward towards the open farmland. Strangely similar he now thought to probably how the moss had spread out across the surfaces of the cave walls. The 425 expansion allowed Danville citizens to live in the country and commute to work downtown, thus the Danville suburbs were born.

He had bought a house out in "The Burbs," as Ham often referred to it...knowing it got under John's skin, right after the 425 was finished. At the time it seemed like a no-brainer. The five-bedroom, four-bath 3700 square foot ranch house was a definite upgrade from the smaller two-bedroom, two-bath apartment he had been renting downtown. The house sat on a six-acre lot that he was especially drawn to at the time - he was looking for some open space. No one to bother him and some peace and quiet from the ever increasingly noisy and congested downtown.

These days he more often than not cursed the decision to buy the house.

His master plan of having a family fill the five-bedrooms had never come to be. And the downtown congestion he had tried to escape by moving out here had now filled in the open space between the city center and the burbs. So now here he was, fighting this damn traffic everyday to and from work.

Work...he thought to himself...that *also* hadn't been part of his master plan.

CHAPTER 19

John still remembers the day he moved in. He inserted the shiny new key into the door lock, feeling the brand new lock tumblers click into place as he turned the key, and he opened the door to his new home. Ham and Mary J had both been there with him to celebrate the big occasion. He couldn't believe his luck at being able to afford such a house. These models were definitely in the top echelon of the Danville real estate market, with the homes in the first phase of the new development selling for almost $600,000.

Each of them had spent their money on different indulgences over the past year. It was amazing what $2,000,000 will buy you in a small Ohio town. Hell, John thought, you could practically buy the town itself!

69

All of them had decided to upgrade their housing, John's ranch being the priciest of the three. John had also bought himself a fully loaded Ford F-250, a truck he had always dreamed of having since being a small boy.

He had good memories of riding in the open bed of his Uncle Buck's F-250 pickup when the family used to visit his southern Ohio farm. Uncle Buck had died from lung cancer just after John turned 12. His uncle had been a die-hard cigarette smoker, he seemed to own an endless supply of shirts and baseball caps that featured the various cigarette company's logos. And die-hard he did in the end from smoking those cancer sticks John thought. He remembers visiting his uncle in the hospital those last few months, and it hadn't been pretty. It had been John's first experience with death and it hit him hard. He had enjoyed the freedom the visits to his uncle's farm brought him. He had spent many hours wandering the open fields rock hunting, every once in a while scaring up a gopher or on a rare occasion finding a fox den. The farm had been sold off after his uncle's death. John guessed that boyhood love of his uncle's farm and the open land were two big reasons why he was immediately drawn to the ranch house.

Ham was more of a muscle-car guy and bought himself a 400 horsepower Shelby Cobra-S and a Chevy Corvette ZR-1. The pair had set him back almost $150 thousand. Add in a very nice fishing boat, decked out with all the latest fish finder and GPS gadgetry, and he topped out his toy buying at just over $200 grand.

John had been a big supporter of the boat purchase since Ham said he could use it whenever he liked. A win-win in John's mind, a brand-new top-of-the-line fishing boat that he didn't have to buy or maintain! As the saying goes, and John believed it to be true, "The two happiest days for a boat owner are the day you buy it and the day you sell it."

Mary J had only splurged on an artsy downtown loft and a four-month all-inclusive European vacation. All in all she was definitely the spendthrift of the three when it came to their newfound wealth.

A common purchase amongst the three had been the motorcycles, it turned out to be a unanimous decision. They'd all agreed the bikes were would be fun, and all three were sold on the cool factor of cruising around Danville on their new cycles.

John bought a Davidson Soft-Tail, Ham a nice Harley Roadster, and Mary J a smaller Harley Street model. John could still remember the look on the face of the Harley Davidson Sales Manager, he could even still remember his name…Steve Robins. Strange…the small seemingly insignificant memories the brain decides to retain. Old Steve just about crapped his pants when the three of them strolled in that afternoon and told him they wanted the bikes and would be paying *cash*. John guessed that Steve was probably still telling that story at holiday dinner parties. Looking back, after all that had happened since that day, it made him feel good to think that he may have done at least a little good. Yep, they had made Steve's day, hell probably his year on just the commission from that day's sale alone!

Everything looked to be going just about perfectly John thought, right up until he'd been bitten...bitten by the gambling bug. He wasn't sure why people called it that, a cruel joke he thought. It made it sound like a small gnat or mosquito, something that could be easily dismissed or brushed off your shirt and squashed. It was more like being run over by the fucking gambling Devil if they ever asked for his opinion.

CHAPTER 20

Whirlwind.

That's the word that best describes the weeks and months that followed "The Discovery." The phrase had been coined by the press and quickly picked up by the people of Danville.

The three had presented the initial sample they'd collected from the cave wall to Mrs. M that next Monday in class. The once vivid green moss had now turned mostly brown in the baggie. Mrs. M held out the plastic bag at arm's reach as she listened to their story. All three were pleading with her to look at it under the classroom's new microscope. After finally convincing her that this wasn't a prank, that she wasn't holding God knows what in the baggie, she promised them to take a look at it after school.

That evening, after the school had quieted down and most of the staff had left for the day, Julie made herself a cup of her favorite herbal green tea and sat down to look at what the kids had brought in. She powered on her new microscope, a Swift M3-B, and prepared the sample mount while it warmed up. She had fought hard to gain the school board's approval to purchase the Swift, and she was proud of her victory. It was a top-notch scope and the kids deserved it.

She worked preparing a dry mount slide sample of the substance from the baggie. She added the cover slip to the slide and re-checked the scope to see if it was ready. Securing the slide on the microscope's stage, she lowered her eyes to the viewer. She slowly adjusted the fine focus until the sample came into clear view. What she saw surprised her. This strange substance appeared to be constructed of multiple interwoven layers. What was especially odd was that the topmost layer was covered with what she could best describe as spore-like clear capsules. She rotated the microscope's turret to increase the magnification to 400X and gasped at what came into view in the eyepiece. The cell structure was star shaped!

She quickly prepared a second slide, a wet mount this time. She took a sample of the material from the clear spore-like capsules and included a live bacteria control specimen. Loading the slide onto the microscope's stage, she returned her eyes to the viewfinder. Julie watched closely as the substance taken from the clear capsules appeared to aggressively attack the stock high school live bacteria specimen. It was unlike anything she had ever seen.

Following her cursory examination, Julie quickly realized that there might be more significance to this new substance than originally thought. She was also quite aware that she was out of her depth when it came to the field of microbiology. With both these thoughts in mind, she decided to contact a close friend of hers, Professor Tim Jorgenson, at The Ohio State University in Columbus.

After cleaning up that night, she emailed him describing the spore-like clear capsules, the strange star cell structure, and the unexpected interaction with the live bacteria specimen. She had typed frantically on the computer keyboard trying to transcribe the night's events into words. As she wrapped up the email, she apologized for being so wordy and ended with "Just excited about what this might turn out to be!?...Julie."

CHAPTER 21

Dr. Timothy Jorgenson had completed his doctorate in microbiology at Georgetown University, graduating at the top of his class. Following graduation two-dozen top tier universities wooed him to lead their microbiology departments. Tim finally chose The Ohio State University, what had finally sealed the deal for Tim coming to OSU had been the dean's promise to give him the freedom to pursue his real passion - cancer research. OSU's big money donors providing nearly unlimited resources, along with their newly built research facilities only made his decision easier.

He had been working the past 18+ years as part of an international team made up of over 100 colleges and universities worldwide. Their mission was the seemingly never-ending quest for the medical field's Holy Grail – the cure for cancer. Over the years he had grown understandably more and more skeptical of the various "Take a look at this - I found it!" emails he received, but he had paused when he saw Julie's email. It had been a while since he'd heard from Julie and the !? made him wonder what she'd stumbled across.

The two had first met at a university fundraiser almost four years ago. She had attended as an OSU alumni and he had been there representing the university's microbiology department. It was easily the least liked part of his job - his once yearly assignment to speak to and socialize with the well-heeled and deep-pocketed alumni and guests the department depended on for funding. The two ran into each other by chance in the hotel bar following the fundraiser's formal dinner and had immediately hit it off.

She immediately recognized him when he sat down on the stool next to her at the bar. She had commented on the speech he'd delivered at the dinner, he had responded back that he'd probably given everyone indigestion talking about bacteria, viruses, and immunology right before their nice filet mignon dinner. After sharing a good laugh, he'd asked if he could buy her another glass of wine. They'd shared a few quips about the merits of merlot versus cabernet and the two of them ended up drinking and talking until last call. The conversation and laughter came so easily that they hadn't even noticed that the adjoining restaurant had cleared out and they'd been left alone at the bar.

It was one of those rare connections you sometimes have in life. You run across another person, a complete stranger in some cases, and once you start talking to them you're shocked to find another person in the world with such common interests and life goals in perfect alignment to your own.

They had talked that night about everything except microbiology and the fundraiser. They'd talked about family (each had two children), husbands and wives (each were on their second), their jobs (while both enjoyed the teaching and academic life they each despised their superiors whom they felt had not earned their positions), and most of all...wine. She preferred the whites, he the reds, and by the end of the night had come to the mildly drunk conclusion that both varietals were pretty damn good.

Since that first conference they had always remained in close email contact. Neither's spouse was aware of the strictly platonic relationship - it had not been by intent, it had just never come up in everyday life conversation. Over the years they'd kept each other updated on what was happening in their lives, both knowing they would be friends for life.

So upon reading Julie's email about her unusual findings, Tim responded that he could make a trip out to see her the following weekend. They could catch up on what was going on in their lives and he would bring along some of the university's laboratory test equipment to take a closer look at the specimen. Although he assumed it would just turn out to be a common fungal spore, he did admit that his interest was piqued by Julie's observations and his trust in her instinct and judgment.

CHAPTER 22

Tim left campus that Friday after his last class and drove down to Danville that evening. Upon arriving, he had a short meet and greet with Ham, John, and Mary J at Julie's house. The three told him about the cave where they had found this strange mossy substance and the bioluminescent glow. They were visibly excited to have a professor from OSU showing interest in their discovery. He spent the remaining time on Saturday and Sunday examining, testing, and re-testing a fresh sample of the substance provided by the teenagers.

Tim had spent his career examining all types of naturally and genetically modified candidates in his and the team's quest to find the silver bullet for cancer. Each time they felt they were on the brink of discovery, with hopes beginning to rise, they were inevitably dashed upon further testing showing the proposed candidates unviability for a myriad of reasons. The primary two failure modes typically being the instability of the candidate or the instability of the host. In layman's terms, the proposed candidate either broke down when exposed to the cancer cells or the proposed candidate ended up killing the patient along with the cancer cells. Overall it had been a very long and frustrating 18+ years. And even though he would never let on to any of his team, he was beginning to lose hope in finding this elusive silver bullet in his lifetime.

That all changed late that Sunday afternoon.

When Tim viewed the first prepared sample from the clear spore capsules under his scope he was astonished to see for himself the star shaped cell structure. Upon initially reading Julie's email, he'd assumed her sample had been cross-contaminated. He'd heard of star cells existing in the brain and spinal cord, but never in a moss or fungal spore specimen.

As he subjected additional samples of the substance inside the clear capsules to the various bacterial samples he brought along with him, he was awestruck at how aggressively the substance neutralized the bacterial sample cells. He couldn't help but notice the slight elevation in his heart rate.

He felt the first thoughts of...*could this be the one?*...start creeping into his head.

Knowing he had to get back to campus for Monday morning classes, Tim reluctantly packed up his gear and returned to Columbus late that Sunday night arriving back just after midnight. Before leaving he pledged to Julie to return the next weekend, bringing with him more sophisticated test equipment and test samples. He didn't mention that one of the samples he planned to return with was the cancer cell C-1A specimen. But his excitement must have shown on his face, with Julie saying, "Soooo I wasn't crazy to call you after all huh!" as they hugged and parted that evening.

CHAPTER 23

Tim struggled to make it through the week's class schedule, wanting to get back to Danville as soon as possible. He'd not felt this level of excitement in a very long time, his brain wrestling with the possibility of the "what if..."

Throughout the week Tim prepared the specimen supplies and test equipment to take back with him, loading it into this Ford Explorer so he wouldn't waste any valuable weekend time packing. He left before dawn that Saturday morning, carrying with him the C-1A specimen. If he had stopped and counted up how many times he'd tested the C-1A specimen against potential cancer cure candidates he guessed the number would have run into the low four digits. He had told himself long ago to stop counting and just keep testing...have faith. But it was damn hard sometimes, and getting harder as the years passed by.

Arriving back in Danville that Saturday morning, he spent the next four hours setting up the test equipment and preparing the C-1A slide specimens. It was well past noon when Tim was finally ready to view the first slide under the scope. He'd brought with him a brand new Nikon N-STORM microscope that the university had just purchased. Tim had been nervous about bringing it since it cost more than most people's houses, but he wanted to be sure of his findings this visit...he couldn't take another week of anticipation. Mounting the slide to the scope's stage, he made the final adjustments to the focus and magnification. He steadied his breathing, as he was taught so long ago in his early research internship days, and lowered his eyes to the binocular eyepiece. He studied the slide sample illuminated under the bright LED lamp.

As he watched, the candidate's star cells seemed to literally seek out and eat the cancerous C-1A cells. He almost couldn't believe what he was seeing! He moved back from the scope and blinked a few times, rubbing his eyes to clear his vision. He then placed his head back to the scope's padded headrest and continued to watch the show playing out below on the microscope's stage. The star cells were avoiding the healthy cells on the slide mount and devouring the C-1A cancer cells. It was unlike anything he had seen over the past 18+ years chasing the cancer cure ghost.

He only realized that he had been holding his breath when he began to feel a bit lightheaded. Tim sat back from the scope, steadying himself and taking in a few deep breaths. Once the lightheadedness had left him, he quickly returned to the scope not wanting to miss a moment.

"Oh my God," he whispered. Smiling as he continued to watch the magical display unfold beneath the scope's lens.

"Oh my God, I've found it!!" he yelled out this time, laughing as he sat back from the scope, both arms raised in the air above his head. "I've found it!"

He repeated the identical experiment four more times. He had to convince himself that what he was seeing was real, not just experimental variation or a result of cross-contaminated specimens.

After hours of preparing, viewing, and repeating the observation process, he sat back in his chair exhausted. It was noon on Sunday, he had been up over 30 hours, but was still wired from the possibility of a breakthrough.

The possibility of *finally* finding cancer's silver bullet.

CHAPTER 24

Danville became an overnight hotspot for the microbiologist community as teams of scientists and academics converged on the town. In the large open field adjacent to Danville High, temporary buildings were erected as laboratories and research facilities. The local Danville rental market turned red hot after the one hotel in town filled up with the influx of personnel associated with the research efforts.

The media followed close behind. Word quickly spread via the local news outlets, and spider-webbed out to state, national, and eventually world news television and Internet sites. The local Danville Channel 7 news story had jumped to CNN and Reuters within 24 hours.

As the days and weeks went by, the interest in the validity of the discovery grew. Corporate

America was beginning to sit up and take notice. It wasn't long before corporate biotech, biomedical, and bioengineering scouts were streaming into Danville. The scout's mission was simple - confirm if the silver bullet had indeed been discovered and if so determine the commercial viability. If the reports proved to be true, then the financial gains could be immense.

Scott Harroll was one such scout. Scott had been sent by Cardiff Technologies, a bioengineering firm headquartered in Palo Alto, California. Cardiff had secured a number of patents over their short 15-year history but had experienced a dry spell as of late. There had been recent rumor talk of possible layoffs or even a shutdown if things didn't pick up in the near future. Scott was Cardiff's top scout, having secured a number of top performing (commercially and financially speaking) products over his 10 years with the company. So when a worried looking Mark Winter, Cardiff's Chief Executive Officer, walked into his office a week ago for a "chat," Scott knew that the rumor talk had more teeth to it then he previously thought.

He'd never met Mark face-to-face, since Mark rarely slummed down to his end of the building. By the end of their 90-minute chat, Scott had a clear understanding of the critical urgency for Cardiff to fill their commercial pipeline. It really wasn't that much of a conversation, since Mark did all the talking after their initial handshake and exchange of professional pleasantries. The message delivered by Mark had been clear, they needed a new financially profitable product…and quickly. Mark's somber face and matter-of-fact wording told the story – it was do-or-die time for the company.

CONVERGENCE

CHAPTER 25

Twenty-three private biotech companies set up shop in and around Danville over those first few weeks after the story went national. Each company brought along their own teams of biotech, bioengineering, and biomedical scientists. Working side-by-side with the company's scientific teams were those from academia. The task was to quickly investigate and research this new cure candidate - the race was on to fine tune the discovery into a safe, commercially viable, product for human consumption.

One such team was the Cardiff Technologies scientific group that Tim Jorgenson worked alongside. Following Tim's initial small-scale trials were Cardiff's first animal trials with the spore capsule substance. These did not go quite as smoothly for the Cardiff team.

The first primate exposure to the spore substance showed "Negative Results." It wasn't until much later, as part of the post-event investigation, what exactly the Cardiff scientists meant by that short two-word conclusion. The onsite trials continued over the next six months as the Cardiff scientists attempted to modify the spore cell structure to ease its recombination with the base animal cell structure system.

During this time period, the chaotic frenzy that had been ignited from the initial information dispersal to the news outlets died off. "The Discovery In Danville," as the news agencies had labeled it, had lost a bit of its shine. And as we all know, it doesn't take long for the viewing public to move on to the next distraction on the evening news or headline on the mainstream Internet news sites.

The first to make their way to the exits and clear out of town were the corporate scouts. The initial report from the scouts to their higher-ups used words and phrases such "Developmental" and "Not commercially or financially viable at this time." And so it wasn't long after that for the scouts, along with their teams of scientists, to be redirected by their corporate boards to move onto the next town or city and next probable pipeline product. It came with the territory, the constant struggle to remain one step ahead of their rivals to bring the next product to the marketplace. So one by one they packed up their gear and left town. The lone exception to this exodus was Scott Harroll.

Scott had been in the scouting business for the entirety of his 33-year career and had developed over that time period what he referred to as his sixth sense. It was his gut feeling, sort of a strange intuition, his version of Spiderman's Spideysense. This sixth sense had made him very successful over his career, as was reflected by the personalized license plate on his Porsche that read 6THSENS. And once again, his gut was telling him to take a pause before packing up his car and heading out of town.

So as all the other firm's scouts and scientists cleared out of town, Scott made a call to Mark Winter to explain the situation and try to convince Mark to give the Cardiff team a little more time. After a brief 30-minute discussion, Scott Harroll hung up the phone and walked down to the lobby of the Danville Motel 6 to extend his stay. His Spideysense alarm gently ringing in the back of his head as the motel manager charged the Cardiff corporate credit card.

Having Tim working alongside the Cardiff team provided Scott a direct connection to Julie McMeekan, and that in turn meant a direct and invaluable connection to Ham, John, and Mary J.

Scott had been introduced to the three during one of his first visits to Danville. From experience, he knew that he had to stay close to these three since they would be the key stakeholders if or when anything did come of this new discovery in terms of commercial viability. They were what were referred to in the corporate scouting business as the "Finders." As with any other business, corporate scouting had its own language. Scott knew these three would need to be "Locked Up," meaning signed under contract quickly if his Spideysense was ringing true. That meant as soon as he was sure the discovery was real and not just another AID's drug or Parkinson's pill that proved to be one more in a long line of false hopes. The optimum lock up result for a scout was to essentially buy off the finders with a single lump sum payment. While this initial lump sum usually appeared quite large and extravagant to the finders, it was typically just a small *fraction* of the full commercial value of the product. A key stipulation buried in the terms and conditions of the lump sum payment contract was that the finders would have to relinquish *all* rights and future profits associated with the product. The lump sum tactic sometimes made Scott feel a bit dirty, but it was just business…at least that's what he always told himself afterwards.

So Scott waited patiently, closely watching the progress of Tim Jorgenson and the Cardiff scientists.

One month.

Two months.

Three months.

All the time his Spideysense alarm ringing steadily in his head, growing just a bit louder with each passing month.

Then came the breakthrough by the Cardiff team.

CHAPTER 26

XR9-2, that was the bioengineer's final formula designator for the engineered solution. After three months, Cardiff's onsite team of scientists had successfully modified the original spore capsule substance's protein DNA strand structure. Shortened to just -2 by the Cardiff team, it was an elegant design with proven stability in the primate testing and the unique innate characteristic to specifically target and destroy cancerous cells. The -2 behaved unlike any previous cure candidate and the research team truly believed they had finally engineered the Holy Grail cure for cancer.

Following a debrief of the amazing progress made by the Cardiff team, Scott Harroll met with Ham, John, Mary J, and their parents the very next weekend to discuss the Cardiff Technologies interest in the rights to their discovery. Of course he didn't divulge the progress the Cardiff scientific team had made with the -2 variant. By dinnertime that Sunday, Scott had the three finders locked up. The lump sum payment cost Cardiff Technologies $6,000,000, $2 million for each finder - Scott conservatively estimated a commercial payback of 500-1000X that amount. He guessed Mark Winter would be *very* happy with that return on investment...he also better be getting more than a card and box of chocolates as a Christmas bonus this year!

The intense national media attention, and eventual national political intervention, allowed Cardiff to run a shortened -2 primate test program - clearing the path for human trials. The FDA officials felt it best to show the nation they had the "public good" at the forefront of their agendas and thus approved the fast-tracked human trial phase. The results were impressive, some might say miraculous. Greater than 95% of the respondents showed positive cancer remission results within the first month of using the -2 treatment.

Mark Winter and the XR9-2 cancer cure treatment made the cover of Time magazine the following month – Cardiff had found their new commercial product line.

CHAPTER 27

A tapping noise broke John from his trance.

"You have a 16 sir, I repeat *again*, do you want to hit or stay?" the dealer was clearly irritated with John's lack of response.

John thought about it for a moment, another goddamned 16, that must have been the fifth or sixth this hour. He made a scratching motion on the felt tabletop with his right hand, indicating he wanted another card at the blackjack table.

Cindy from Idaho, as her standard casino issued nametag indicated, pulled the next card from the six deck auto-shuffling shoe. In a well-practiced fluid motion, she slid and flipped over the card adding it to the ones in front of John. A king of spades.

"26," she said robotically as she gathered up his cards along with the stack of black $100 chips. $700 more...gone.

The casino was almost empty at this 3 a.m. hour on a Tuesday night...well Wednesday morning really. He glanced down at his TAG Heuer watch, about 15 hours he'd been at it. He'd been playing a combination of blackjack, poker, and craps, even though blackjack was his go-to game. That $700 put him in the hole just over $170 thousand.

John's first experience with the riverboat gambling scene came right after the Cardiff Technologies payout, or *payoff* was more like it now in his mind. The three of them had decided to try it out over a weekend to escape the media, family, and friend's attention, and to celebrate their newfound wealth.

The casino boats, docked on the Mississippi river, were a short two-hour drive from Danville down Interstate 71. Of course they really weren't boats. They were essentially brick and mortar casinos with a riverboat façade to draw in the tourists. On board they walked, wide-eyed and mesmerized by the array of flashing neon lights and ringing one-armed bandit machines. Buying into the belief that they were boarding a majestic riverboat from bygone days. When really, once you were through the front door, you could have been in any Atlantic City or Las

Vegas stuffy, smoky, clock and window free casino. The interiors were all business with one specific goal – separate the money from the players.

His first few trips had been amazing, the kind you tell stories about to your buddies. He still remembered the feeling of that adrenaline rush from his first big win. His heart racing, a bit lightheaded, a feeling like he owned the world...it seemed so easy, *too* easy. He had often wondered since that time if it was similar to that feeling when a person first tries crack cocaine. He'd read about it in some magazine, how it was such an intense high and feeling of power that the user was hooked from their very first use...that was the case with John and gambling.

$127,540...his total winnings from that first big weekend - he had bought the TAG watch that weekend in celebration. And he was hooked ever since...*his* crack cocaine.

John had always been a firm believer in the old saying "You've got to have money to make money" and his $2 million Cardiff payout allowed him to bet big...real big. He had quickly transitioned from the $10 and $25 tables to making $1,000-$2,000 bets per blackjack or poker hand or craps dice roll. You throw in the occasional $10-$20 thousand bet when he was feeling especially lucky, and the money either came in or went out at a very fast pace.

"Sir?"

"Sir?"

Tonight he was visiting the riverboat casino The Queen Mary, bearing no resemblance to the famous ocean liner. Tonight's dealer of choice was Cindy from Idaho. Cindy who was once again was trying to bring John's attention back to the blackjack table.

John was the lone player at the $100 minimum bet table. Others had come and gone throughout the night and early morning. He thought of himself as the lone survivor...or as that small voice told him in his head, maybe just the lone idiot to still be trying and losing at it for this long.

"Sir...are you betting?" Cindy from Idaho broke through the alcohol-induced fog in his brain.

"Cindy, what do you think I should do?" John asked - already knowing what her response would be.

In her very well practiced and robotic voice Cindy responded as expected, "Sir, we are not allowed to advise players." Too bad he couldn't have bet on her response he thought, he would have finally been a winner tonight.

"Fuck it!" John blurted out, pushing the remainder of his chips that were in front of him onto the blackjack betting circle.

"Sir, please watch your language or I will have to ask you to..." Cindy sternly started to say.

"Just deal the goddamned cards!" John snapped back cutting her off mid-sentence.

Cindy placed her hand on the six-deck shoe shuffling box and made a slight back and forth flip motion. Her signal to the eye in the sky camera mounted directly overhead in the casino ceiling, one of the 20 or so that were blanketing the casino tables, that she might need some security assistance with a player at her table. The hand motion was imperceptible to all but the most professionally trained. John paid no attention, but the security team sitting in the casino's back room confines immediately picked up on the hand signal. They radioed the pit boss through his earpiece, who then casually strolled over to Cindy's table to see what was going on. All of this took place in just a few minutes.

When the pit boss arrived, Cindy reported that she had warned John about his language and then also noted to him the very large all-in bet that John had just placed. The pit boss on duty, Curt Hyde, acknowledged the bet size and then took position beside and slightly behind Cindy. He then quickly squeezed the pager button he had cupped in his right hand palm, three quick taps. The triple reply signaled the security team that he had arrived at the table and was comfortable managing the situation. It also signaled them to redirect an additional camera to record the table play as evidence in case the guest continued to show aggressive behavior, or worst case, it escalated to physical confrontation and removal from the casino. The casino's camera recording would also be reviewed for any possible cheating, since John's current bet size automatically triggered the casino's protocol requiring a secondary camera review.

Curt was pretty sure John was not cheating. He'd seen John in the casino numerous times in the past and was quite familiar with John's luck at cards and dice, most all of it was bad. He was more concerned with whether or not John would hold it together when he finally lost. Curt had seen John's type a hundred times before, and it was really just a matter of time before his luck ran out. Curt was looked upon within the casino's pit team as the best among them at reading the "guests," or as they joked among themselves in the back room on breaks, the "depositors." More often than not, the guests deposited whatever money they brought before leaving the casino.

He'd been keeping an eye on John since he came on shift. He recognized him from the backroom cameras and had been debriefed of the situation from the second shift pit boss – "John had been losing big and drinking big." Not the best recipe for a quiet third shift for Curt.

In the three hours Curt had been on shift, John had put away four Budweiser's along with five shots of Patron tequila. The beer didn't worry him…the tequila was a different story. Tequila in his experience made people brave, *stupidly* brave, which always meant trouble for him.

Over his career working the pit, Curt had seen this same story played out over and over. In his early years he remembered feeling sorry for some of the players, now he was pretty much numb to the feeling. He'd long since realized the disease of gambling was alive and well, seeing first hand how it completely and utterly took over and controlled some people. Curt watched John at the table nervously flipping his cards about in front of him. He saw that desperate out-of-fucking-control look written all over his face, reflected back in his beer, tequila, and casino smoke bloodshot eyes.

He steadied himself beside Cindy, shifting his weight from foot to foot to keep alert. He studied John while running various "guest removal" scenarios through his mind in case he had to react, and react quickly.

Cindy methodically re-sorted and re-stacked the black $100 and green $500 chips in nice little piles in front of John's betting circle that contained his cards. As taught, she intentionally took a little longer to complete the sorting and stacking process, trying to diffuse the situation.

"$37,900 is the bet," she announced. She waited for the pit boss to reconfirm her count, and also ok the bet since it was over the maximum table limit bet of $10,000.

Curt only needed a few seconds to run the chip count in his head, but also took his time knowing from experience that it was best to slow down these types of situations. He voiced an "Approved" to Cindy, who had turned to face him awaiting his go-ahead.

Cindy could feel the tension build as she scanned John and readied herself to pull the next card from the six-deck shoe.

"C'mon Cindy!" John shouted out, a bit agitated at the delay in the action. He was now standing up in anticipation of the first card out of the shoe, "Be nice to me for once tonight!"

Cindy slid the first card out. "Ace of diamonds," she reported as she slid the card in front of John, centering it within his betting circle.

"Hell yes!" John shouted out. He felt a surge of adrenaline pulse through his system. It had been a long while since he'd felt it, and it felt good. This was where it all turned around, John told himself. I'll win my money back and walk away, maybe even call it quits for good on the gambling. He repeated this to himself in his mind a few times and it sounded nice…but he'd told himself this lie many times in the past.

"I will this time!" John yelled. He had been so lost in his thoughts he mistakenly shouted it out.

"Excuse me sir, are you alright?" Curt questioned. John's outburst had caught him off guard, he was now beginning to get worried where this situation might end up and could see the nervous look in Cindy's eyes after the strange comment.

"Yeah, yeah, I'm fine," said John.

At that moment, the casino suddenly seemed to come into vivid focus for John. The lights seemed to brighten and the one-arm bandit bell sounds seemed to sweeten. His beer and tequila clouded mind suddenly becoming clear.

Cindy continued with her methodical dealing. The next card out of the shoe was a nine of hearts; she slid it over in front of and on top of the ace already in his betting circle. She paused, straightening both cards perfectly in front of John.

"That's what I'm *fucking* talking about!" John shouted. He reached forward and pounded the table, his fists coming down hard enough topple over a few of Cindy's neat chip stacks.

Curt quickly moved around from behind the table, positioning himself next to John, and placed his hand on John's arm. He leaned down and spoke slowly and clearly into John's ear, "Sir, I will remove you from the casino if you use that sort of language again." Curt's large hand seemed to engulf John's arm and he gave it a slight squeeze to make sure he had John's full attention.

John instinctively pulled his arm away, barely acknowledging the pit boss's presence. He felt like he owned this casino at the moment, and wasn't going to let some $20 an hour pit boss ruin it for him.

"Relax...I got it, I got it!" he barked back to Curt.

The shouting and commotion had drawn in other casino guests to the table, all of them wanting to get a front row seat to the action. It was just human nature showing its face once again, bringing out the curious on-lookers. Like drivers on the freeway that slow to look at a car crash, people always like to see someone in worse-off shape than themselves.

Cindy paused and stood motionless behind the table, happy to allow Curt handle the situation. She finally stepped back to the table and readied herself to deal the cards for the house hand. She quickly drew two cards in succession from the shoe. The first card she placed face down, the second she turned face up and slid it on top. A six of hearts.

A smile slowly spread across John's face. The odds were now most definitely in his favor, the dealer was showing a classic bust hand. The books, the statistics, the experts, everyone will tell you that the odds were she had a 10 spot card under that six, giving her a 16 and leading her to bust 21 hand.

Cindy motioned to John asking him if he wanted another card on top of his ace-nine soft 20.

"Yeah right, in your dreams. Hell no!" John snapped back, "You've got a bust hand!" He could feel the confidence well up inside him. "Let's see what you have Cindy-girl," John continued.

Cindy proceeded to turn over her bottom card and slide it into place next to the six of hearts. It was an ace of clubs; she had a seven or soft 17. Following the casino rules imprinted onto the blackjack's felt tabletop stating "Dealer Must Hit On Soft 17," Cindy prepared to draw the next card from the shoe. She slid the card out and placed it face up in line with her other two cards, it was a nine of clubs

"16," Cindy announced.

John rose from the table, his heart raced into the next gear, this was playing out perfectly. He had been a little worried by Cindy's ace, but she had re-dug her hole and was right back at a bust 16 hand. But this time it was a hard 16, nowhere for her to hide now. Once again his mind ran through the odds of her busting and everything was in his favor.

Cindy paused once more to collect her thoughts before pulling what she also assumed would be a bust card for her.

Her hand moved slowly over the face of the shoe and withdrew the next card. Sliding it across the felt she turned it over to join the three cards in front of her…it was a five of diamonds.

"21," she reported calmly.

Time seemed to slow as Cindy moved the final card into position. John could see her speaking, but couldn't hear any of her words. He'd done the simple math, he knew the number, and he knew what it meant. Cindy's hand was now reaching out to gather up his chip stacks. John said nothing. He slowly sank back into his chair, staring ahead in disbelief.

It was over.

***

The next morning John walked into River's Pawnshop, located conveniently next to the Queen Mary casino, and dropped his Harley keys on the counter. After a brief 15-minute negotiation with Frank River who owned the pawnshop, the two settled on a value of $4,500 for the motorcycle. Negotiation was probably too strong a word for what had taken place during those short 15 minutes, with

John essentially capitulating to Frank's offer. During the negotiations Frank had also taken notice of the TAG watch on John's wrist.

"I'll make it an even $5,000 if you throw in the watch."

"I'm keeping the *fucking* watch, just give me the forty-five hundred," John angrily responded.

"A damn thief!" is what John yelled back at Frank over his shoulder as he exited the pawnshop, stuffing the cash into his pocket.

"Thank you for your business, come again," was all Frank replied as he tossed the Harley keys from hand to hand. Guys like John were a dime a dozen. He'd seen hundreds of his type stumble into the shop since he'd opened. Prior night's bad luck gamblers parting with family heirlooms and near-and-dear to the heart keepsakes. The casino's effectiveness at parting gamblers from their money meant a steady business for the pawnshop owner.

After leaving the pawnshop, John walked to the bus station and bought a one-way Greyhound bus ticket home to Danville that evening.

CHAPTER 28

Cardiff Technologies was looked upon by most in Danville as a blessing for the town. And why not, prior to Cardiff planting stakes in the ground the average income in Danville was a hair above the national poverty level of $23,850 for a family of four. Cardiff brought with them a wide variety of jobs and advancement opportunities never before seen in Danville. These jobs opened the middle and upper middle class doors to many citizens of Danville that prior to Cardiff, would never had even seen the door itself.

Within three years of Cardiff setting up shop in Danville, the average income had risen to more than $45,000. This increase had mostly come over the past two years due to the infusion of high paying jobs surrounding the production expansion of the

XR9-2 treatment. The Danville Cardiff site grew to almost 4000 people, running a three shift, seven days a week operation. While many citizens of Danville benefited from the new Cardiff employment opportunities, a large percentage of the 4,000-person workforce was hired from outside Danville due to the specific technical skill requirements. The majority of these new Danville'ites lived within the city limits or in close proximity in the nearby suburbs.

New jobs ranged from entry-level shipping and receiving/handling technicians, to senior level executive positions. The most senior level positions reporting directly to the site Vice President who in turn reported to Cardiff's CEO Mark Winter.

Yes...Cardiff Technologies coming to town was a godsend.

CHAPTER 29

The five and a half hour, six aspirin, Greyhound bus ride back to Danville was a sobering experience for John compared to the trip out on his Harley. It provided him ample time to nurse his hangover from the previous night's gambling and drinking binge and contemplate what he was going to do with the rest of his life. It also provided him the opportunity to learn about all the intricacies of needlepoint from Edith.

He forgot Edith's last name…Wentworth…or maybe it was Wentridge, something close to that, who sat beside him in row 19. He had intentionally chosen a window seat on the bus thinking it would provide him with some privacy, at least no neighbor on one side, and a window to rest his throbbing head against. Just his luck when he saw the elderly lady coming down the bus aisle way. He kept repeating to himself in his head "Please not by me, please not by me, please not by..." as she took the seat next to his.

She immediately introduced herself and proceeded to give John an in depth training session on needlepoint, specifically her expertise with the continental stitch. He was just starting to have thoughts of...This is why people murder others out of the blue with seemingly no connections, when she had dozed off. She'd been sleeping soundly the past two hours. Thank You God! John thought smiling.

Of course without having Edith to think or complain about, his thoughts drifted back to the issue at hand in his life - he was flat broke. He still couldn't wrap his head around it, he was worse than broke; he was two months behind on his ranch house mortgage. He had paid cash for the house, but had refinanced twice. He was now the proud owner of a 30-year mortgage at not the most favorable interest rate. The refinances had provided the cash to fuel his riverboat gambling trips. Thinking back on the whole mess caused his stomach to take another flip. Adding to his nausea was the alcohol that was ever so slowly and painfully working its way through his system.

About the only thing of value he still owned outright was his Ford F-250, he hadn't traded in that pink slip...at least not yet.

CONVERGENCE

"Broke...broke...broke," John repeated as he looked out the window at the Ohio farmland outside passing by in a blur. His head gently vibrating against the Greyhound's window only adding to his headache, and the smell of the bus's toilet two rows back only compounding his nausea. Edith had now settled into a peaceful snore next to him. As John listened to her, he once again walked back through the twists and turns he had taken in his life to end up here on bus 553, seat 19A, next to needlepoint expert Edith.

CHAPTER 30

John needed a job and he knew he wasn't exactly the poster child of a highly skilled or experienced worker. His life resume to date would read something like this…

- Bag boy at the Danville Market
- Danville High graduate
- One of the famous Danville Three
- Rich beyond belief
- Flat broke and unemployed

It was painfully obvious that he would have to rely on those 15 minutes of fame for being one of the Danville Three to move on from here. There wasn't a whole hell of a lot else to lean upon.

Greyhound 553 pulled into Danville late that Sunday night around 11 p.m. A light drizzle began to fall as John stepped off the bus, the temperature hovering around the 50-degree mark. Fall was definitely on its way if it hadn't already come to town. The weather further dampened John's mood as he walked from the bus into the downtown terminal. He wandered over to the window marked "Taxi Service" and knocked on the cracked Plexiglass to let the taxi hailer know he had a customer. A "How in the hell did I end up in this job?" 45ish looking, unshaven man slowly swung around on his stool. He was not at all pleased to be pulled away from the fuzzy screened 13-inch TV set showing what looked to be an old black and white western movie. After reserving a taxi with the man, who didn't speak a single word during the process – just grunted his acknowledgement of the transaction, John took a seat in the terminal and waited for the taxi to arrive.

The 30-minute taxi ride home gave John time to think about whom he could call for a job. The list wasn't long. He decided his best shot was an old friend he graduated with from Danville High, Tom Simmons. He had heard a while back that Tom now worked at the new Cardiff Technologies plant as a lab supervisor.

He and Tom had been buddies throughout high school and John had always considered him a close friend, second only to Ham. After the Discovery, he had lost contact with Tom, as he had with pretty much everyone else in his life other than Ham and

Mary J. He had proven not to be the most gracious friend when it came to his newfound fame and wealth. While he couldn't remember having intentionally snubbed Tom along the way, he wouldn't be surprised if Tom told him to "Go to hell!" once he got him on the phone asking for a job. Oh had the tables turned.

So John hoped for the best but expected the worst when he rang Tom the following morning. Much to his amazement and relief, after a bit of catching up and reminiscing of the good old times back at Danville High, Tom quickly offered up an entry-level lab assistant position he had open on his team. He didn't even ask the obvious and indefensible question along the lines of "Why does a multimillionaire need a $15 a hour job?" He was grateful...extremely grateful. John didn't know how he would have responded if Tom started asking questions about what had happened, he probably would have just hung up on him. John realized he needed to come up with a story about what had happened...and soon.

"Come by next Monday," was all Tom had said, "and we'll talk."

"Thanks, I *really* appreciate it," was John's response, and he truly did.

CONVERGENCE

After John hung up the receiver, he wondered if Tom had sensed the desperation and the "I'm at the end of my rope" resignation tone in his voice.

Tom sat in his kitchen across town staring dumbfounded at the phone receiver in his hand…he'd heard it.

CHAPTER 31

Those first few months for John at Cardiff were uncomfortable to say the least. He had survived the initial barrage of questions from both his new co-workers as well as from friends and family. He'd been vague with his explanation of what had happened to him over the past year. The story usually centered on making bad investment decisions and taking money advice from the wrong people. He could see the "I told you so" look in their eyes as they listened to his story. And even though everyone was empathetic to his situation, he thought he could also see that most were somewhat happy he'd lost it all and been brought back to ground zero. It was base human nature once again shining through. We are envious of those who hit it big, be it the lottery (or being in the right cave at the right time

- John smiled as he thought about that), but secretly we are also happy to see them then lose it all. It's that little bit of evil in all of us, residing in the deepest marrow of the human soul, that takes pleasure in seeing someone fall from the top and end up back clawing for their day-to-day existence with the rest of the human populace.

The only people John told the whole truth to were Ham and Mary J. After he had settled into his new job, he'd called and invited them to dinner, something he hadn't done in a long time...and told them the entire story.

The money.
The gambling.
The drinking.
The fall.

It was a classic tale really, just not as romantic or glamorous as they portray on the big screen or write about in the bookstore novels. In the movies there was always the sure-fire ticket selling equation of the overly attractive leading character + booze + gambling + parties = leading character's demise and eventual bottoming out. John felt cheated, he had gone from the booze + gambling to bottoming out, and missed the party piece in between. In real life it had proven to be a much more painful story, one in which he wished he *weren't* the leading character.

CONVERGENCE

CHAPTER 32

John's mind was racing with emotions as he sat at the traffic light. He was happy to be through with dinner and out of Chili's...feeling like he could breathe again, but unsure what to do next.

He glanced again over at the 3-by-12 inch shiny metallic box sitting beside him on the F-250's bench seat. The sound of the rain was now growing louder on the truck's cab roof. "A classic crisp fall day was on tap! No rain in sight!" the cheery Channel 7 weathercaster Todd Pritchard had reported that Saturday morning while John watched the news drinking his morning coffee. What the fuck did Mr. Pritchard know! He pictured ol' Todd sitting in his air conditioned newsroom, not a care in the world except to make sure he pasted the right goddamned picture of the smiling or frowning sun on the greenscreen map of Ohio. Well he had sure gotten it wrong today, "Should have pasted that frowning sun up there today Todd-O" John said, trying to get his mind off the box...and off of tonight's dinner conversation.

"Com'on light...any day now would be nice" John said.

He wiped his arm across his rain-dampened forehead. He couldn't stop himself from looking over and checking on the box. His brain first telling him that he was crazy and should turn the truck around now and return it, then quickly flip-flopping and telling him that he was out of options - this was his *only* option, his *only* out, even though his chances of success were slim at best. He had a mental image flash through his head – his situation was like one of those TV commercials where the actor has a Devil on one shoulder and an angel on the other trying to convince the person to do their bidding. Staring at the box, his eyes were naturally drawn to the red biohazard warning symbol laser engraved on its shiny rectangular lid.

The traffic light finally turned from red to green and John accelerated to merge onto the freeway, blending into the Saturday night traffic. His truck quickly becoming one of the many cars marching eastbound along the 425. He wasn't sure where he was going, but at least it felt good to be moving again.

CHAPTER 33

Ham and Mary J sat next to each other in the booth across from John at the Chili's restaurant. It was just past 4 p.m. and the restaurant was still fairly empty, the Saturday dinner crowd just starting to filter in. The waitress had sat them in a booth towards the back of the restaurant. They listened in quiet disbelief as John told his story about what had happened over the past year.

They both had often wondered how things were going with John. He had been the topic of many conversations during their weekly visits to The Percolator, an old hole in the wall coffee shop in downtown Danville. Neither had heard from him in many months, which wasn't like John. The three had been just about inseparable up to and through the Discovery and Cardiff payout time period. Then about three months after the payout, John seemed to just drop off the grid and vanish from their lives. Ham had reached out to him several times, leaving him numerous voicemails but had never gotten a response. He felt like he was being given the cold shoulder and finally stopped calling, he could take a hint. It crossed his mind if the money truly had changed John, but he always gave John the benefit of the doubt and chalked it up to him just having some fun – probably just enjoying his newfound wealth.

"You should have come to us for help," Ham finally said, breaking the silence after John finished with his story. He was stunned - he really didn't know what to say. After hearing everything that John had just told the two of them over the past hour he felt like he was looking at a complete stranger across the table from him. Ham thought about offering him money, but quickly reconsidered. He figured John would either say "Thanks, but no thanks" or more likely just be immediately insulted, only making matters worse.

John immediately sensed their uneasiness after he had finished talking and tried to smooth out the situation.

"I'm not telling you all of this to ask for money," he said, "I screwed up...I screwed up *big* time. I need to own up to that and see what I can do to get my life back on the rails. I just needed to tell someone the whole truth."

They finished their meals in an awkward silence. Ham and Mary J continuing to process what they had just heard while John was beginning to have the first pangs of regret for telling them. He could already feel and see that their relationship had changed over these past few hours. They were already looking at him differently. From the good friend that they'd shared crazy Danville High trials and tribulations with, to someone that needed help, someone to feel sorry for, someone to take pity on. That last part hit him hard in the gut.

John felt more alone than ever.

The waitress finally dropped the bill off to the table and Mary J quickly reached over and snatched it up. "I've got this," she blurted out, "my treat." Her first words since John had finished with his story.

She welcomed the relief of having something, anything, to say completely off subject. She glimpsed over to the exit door feeling herself wanting to get out of the restaurant and into the cool night air. Get home, have a glass or two of wine, maybe half the bottle after this evening, and try to understand how someone she thought she knew so well had vanished in front of her eyes.

CHAPTER 34

Aside from the uncomfortable questions, John's first week at Cardiff went surprisingly well. He actually felt as if he made a few new friends, the first time probably since high school. He kept his head down and concentrated on learning the ins and outs of what it took to be a lab technician. It surprised him, but it felt good to be back in the mix of everyday life, even if it was for only $15.25 an hour.

He was assigned to the quality control department. This meant his group completed the final check to ensure that the product currently being produced met or exceeded the FDA and other governing regulatory agency standards and requirements. The group viewed themselves as the

Cardiff police, making sure all the rules were being followed.

He had to admit, he was actually enjoying the work. It had been nearly six years since he'd actually had a real job, and this was definitely a big step up from bag boy at the Danville Market. He'd forgotten what it felt like to put in a full day's work and go home tired at night. Tired but actually feeling proud of a job well done.

***

It was during the second month at Cardiff that he found out about Ham and Mary J, after meeting them that Saturday night at Chili's. The same night he stopped off at the Third Base Tavern on his way home, his first drinks in over a month…his first since hitting rock bottom with Cindy's damn four-card 21 on the Queen Mary.

CONVERGENCE

CHAPTER 35

After the initial Discovery, a whirlwind of attention enveloped the three friends. Everything changed. Everyday strangers they passed on the street now wanted to catch up on old times, stop and chat, or take a quick picture with them. The instant celebrity, even in Danville, Ohio, brought along with it unexpected stress and anxiety. The bright spotlight of attention from the media drove the three to retreat to the confines of their friendship for common understanding and safety, away from the chaos that engulfed the town.

They withdrew from everyday Danville life around town, stopped going out in the public unless absolutely necessary, and turned to one another for support. The three experienced similar feelings to that of survivors from a psychologically traumatic incident. That common saying of "You can't understand unless you've been there and experienced what I've gone through" applied. It turned out being famous wasn't all fun and games like they thought it would be.

For that short period of time they essentially lived together, hanging out and sleeping over at each other's places to avoid going out and having to deal with the media and public. They confided in one another about their dreams, worries, and fears brought on by their sudden fame and fortune.

It was also during this time that Ham and Mary J began to fall in love.

CONVERGENCE

CHAPTER 36

As quickly as the whirlwind of attention blew into town it blew out. The press corps and media outlets were smart enough to understand the life cycle of a story. From their experience, when the viewing public started showing signs of boredom with a story, it was time to redirect their interest elsewhere to support the ratings. So as the luster wore off the Danville Discovery story, the news outlets redirected their reporters, camera crews and circus train of support vans and equipment to the next bright and shiny object of media distraction.

As the focused attention on the three of them died down, they naturally started to drift apart and back to their normal lives. John found various distractions to spend his time and money on and eventually, as they now knew, to *lose* his money on.

At the same time Ham and Mary J began to gravitate back towards each other, eventually falling in love as the weeks and months passed by.

There had already been a mutual attraction between the two. The onslaught of unwanted media attention driving all three of them into close quarters only strengthened the relationship between Ham and Mary J. Over the following six months their feelings for one another deepened. And then, during one of their regular weekly visits to The Percolator for coffee, Mary J finally slid a spare loft key across the table Ham – he moved in the next day. They were incredibly happy together, and why not...they had all the money they would ever need, double in fact with their combined take away from the Cardiff payout. They didn't have to work, spent most of those early days in bed, and the remainder of their time drinking coffee at The Percolator and planning getaway trips on their new motorcycles. While John was always in the back of their minds, he was exactly that, taking a backseat to their newfound relationship and time together.

Ham proposed a month later and they were happily married the following spring.

During this time period they lost all contact with John. No calls, no emails, no texts for almost the entire year. Through mutual friends they heard some rumors around gambling and drinking, but had

always assumed that even if true the John they knew
had it under control.

CHAPTER 37

Ham and Mary J had planned to tell John about their marriage that Saturday night at Chili's. They thought it would be just another reason to celebrate as the three friends reunited to reminisce about old times and talk about what they'd been up since they'd last seen each other. Ham was also going to surprise John with his recent town treasurer election victory and maybe start making plans for the two of them to try out Ham's new boat on those prime LLF spots. But sitting there stunned after listening to John's story, they both knew the announcements would have to wait.

It wasn't until leaving the restaurant, when Ham reached out and grabbed Mary J's hand calling her "Honey," that John realized their relationship had grown beyond friendship. He had been so focused on telling his story, finally spilling out the truth to someone...almost not able to wait to rid himself of the weight he'd been carrying around his neck, that he completely missed the matching wedding bands. Now he could just make out a glimmer of gold on her finger, the Chili's parking lot lights intermittently reflecting off the wedding band as they walked together back to their car.

Just perfect, John thought. He was broke and they were happily married *and* rich twice over! He felt a wave of jealousy sweep over him. Things just seem to be getting better and better, he sarcastically thought as he watched Ham and Mary J drive off into the night.

There was just a hint of a mist now coming down. John closed his eyes and turned his face upwards to the night sky, the tiny water droplets slowly coating his face. Why not he thought, bring on the rain God and further dampen an otherwise shitty evening. He stood there, still in the middle of the parking lot, his face now wet from the mist. A loud blare from a car horn made him slowly open his eyes. He looked down in time to see another satisfied Chili's customer trying to leave the parking lot and clearly annoyed at having to swerve to miss him. He could just make out the driver shouting inside his car through the rolled up window, voicing his displeasure with John as he passed. For a brief moment John actually wished the driver had run him down.

He finally turned and walked back to his truck, his face now dripping and jacket wet from the mist turned to light rain. Feeling mentally exhausted from the evening, John climbed into the F-250's cab and sat listening to the rain falling on the cab's roof. He left the radio off - he didn't think he could process any more local bad news or dear God even worse, listen to some down and out country song that might just push him over the edge. He turned the ignition key and started the truck, then steered it out of the Chili's parking lot and towards his over mortgaged ranch house. Nothing but the phlit-phlit-phlit sound from the windshield wipers and the noise of the truck's wet tires skimming across the roadway filling the cab.

As he drove eastbound on the 425 he replayed the night's dinner conversation with Ham and Mary J. He could feel his heart rate increase as the bitter resentment of their happiness rose to the surface.

His own fondness of Mary J had grown from those first few days exploring the cave. They had become very close, at least looking back in *his* mind, in the months that followed, exploring the cave system and then afterwards when the three of them took refuge from the limelight of the press onslaught. But it turns out while they were growing closer as friends, Ham and Mary J had been falling in love.

And if you consider that fact that he essentially dropped out of her life over the past year…well…he knew he could only blame himself and he should be happy for them.

His emotions flip-flopped as he told himself that's how life is, win some lose some. But in John's mind he was always on the latter while Ham seemed to always end up on the winning side. It was damn hard not to feel a touch of jealousy and resentment towards Ham. As hard as he fought to keep the feelings down, they kept rising back up to the surface. Like bile in his throat that he had to fight to swallow back down each time.

Traffic was beginning to stack up on the freeway ahead of him, the 425 was not much of a freeway these days. He reflected back on when he first moved to the outskirts of town, driving home at night he would be lucky to see more than a handful of cars along the way.

John's mind was swirling with thoughts and emotions – resentment, jealousy, hate, self-pity, and self-doubt. His favorite watering hole from his recently given-up drinking and gambling life, the Third Base Tavern, was a couple exits further up. He used to be a nightly regular at the tavern. His head began to ache as he wrestled to calm the emotional turmoil. It also began to ache, no *thirst*, for him to make a stop at the Third Base. He could feel his heart beating in his chest, as he became hyperaware of the upcoming decision point to exit the freeway or keep driving. The reflective exit sign was just illuminating in the F-250 headlamps. He gripped the wheel tightly and the truck slowly veered off the 425 onto the exit ramp.

John pulled into the Third Base Tavern parking lot at just after 7 p.m. that Saturday evening. He grabbed the shiny metallic case off the passenger side seat and opened it quickly to convince himself the -1 vile was still safely inside...it was, safe and sound. He closed the box, looking once more at the red symbol engraved on its cover, and slid it under his side of the bench seat. It made him feel a little better having it out of sight. "Out of sight, but not out of mind," he thought was how the saying went. He hoped a few drinks might fix that that last part.

Getting out of the truck he glanced around the parking lot, it was still fairly empty. He imagined the rain was probably keeping the casual drinkers at home and the hardcore Saturday night drinking crowd had yet to roll in. Entering the bar, he was comforted by the familiar sights, sounds and smells. Nothing had changed during his absence over the past few months, it was as if he had never left. His mixed feelings of doubt, shame, and failure for stopping in were quickly driven down in his psyche by the overwhelming thirst for a drink. He told himself he *deserved* it after what he'd been through this evening at dinner, just one drink to calm his nerves and then he'd head home. A lie he knew deep down. A familiar self-justification he was sure every alcoholic had told him or herself along the way. He knew he didn't deserve a drink, he knew what his mind was telling him, and he knew why he so desperately wanted to buy into the lie - human nature truly was a bitch. He was keenly aware of all the reasons not to be in the tavern, but nonetheless there he stood looking at his reflection in the long Budweiser mirror that covered the entire wall behind the bar.

Fuck it, he thought to himself, and took a position at the end of the bar. He ordered up a double Jack Daniels & Coke...his go-to drink.

CHAPTER 38

John barely tasted the drink as he sipped at it. Tonight's conversation at Chili's with Ham and Mary J, along with wrestling with the decision about what to do with the shiny metallic box under his front seat, had his head spinning. It reminded him of how he felt after riding the Ferris wheel at the Danville Fall Carnival.

As a child he loved to go to the carnival. It was magical to him - the lights, the sounds, and the somewhat scary carnival workers standing next to the rides and outside the mirrored fun houses. He had always preferred the Ferris wheel to those fun houses as a kid. A simpler time he longed for as he now sat at the bar. He closed his eyes and pictured the Ferris wheel in his mind; the wheel slowly spinning around with him positioned at the ride controls. He listened to the excited kid's chatter as they stood in line. He took the next passenger's ticket and loaded them into the cars as they stopped at the bottom of the cycle. At least they *should* stop, he *should* be able to control the speed, and there *should* be riders in line waiting excitedly to get on the ride. But the ride in his mind didn't have a line filled with giggling children eating cotton candy and caramel apples. He was alone at the controls, and no matter how he tried to stop or slow the wheel it just kept on spinning, faster, and faster. As he watched the cars go past he recognized a few of the faces. He saw Ham and Mary J, he even saw himself in one car holding up a bottle of Jack Daniels, almost like he was toasting himself as the car whizzed past at the lowest point on its path. The next car was empty, or at least he thought it was as he watched it lower into view. But there, sitting on the car's seat was the metallic box...just like the one sitting under his F-250's bench seat in the parking lot. As the car passed by John, he could just make out the gleaming red symbol on its shiny cover.

He quickly blinked open his eyes and shook his head, trying to clear the images from his mind. His drink sat half full on the bar in front of him - he reached for it and shot the rest down in a single gulp. The cool drink felt good going down his throat, he could just start to feel the familiar fog of the alcohol spread across his mind. It felt like a warm blanket covering his doubts, worries, anxieties…and those images of the damn Ferris wheel. His head, which had been clouded and aching before entering the bar wrestling with the decision of whether or not to continue on with the plan to sell the -1 vile in parallel with trying its best to process Ham and Mary J's relationship, was feeling better now as the alcohol started to deaden his senses.

He motioned to the bartender for another.

CHAPTER 39

Walking out of Cardiff Technologies with the XR9-1 vile had been much easier than John ever anticipated.

He'd spent weeks planning out how to get his hands on the XR9-1. He still wasn't even sure what it was since all he knew of it he'd learned through lunch table conversations. In the end, it was his notoriety and 15 minutes of fame that sealed the deal and allowed him to walk out of Cardiff with the metallic box containing the -1 vile tucked into the pocket of his jeans.

It was during his first week at Cardiff that John became aware of the -1 variant strain of the XR9-2 cancer cure. The subject had been brought up during lunch conversations with his coworkers. After helping him get the job, Tom Simmons had taken John under his wing, introducing him around the plant that first week and inviting him to join their lunch table. John thought it probably wasn't just because Tom had a big heart that he volunteered to help him out. He imagined Tom's social standing at Cardiff Technologies could only benefit by showing he was a close friend with one of the famous Danville Three.

One of the regulars at the lunch table was Paul Travers, a friend of Tom's who worked in the Research and Development lab. Paul had brought up the -1 strain subject one afternoon while giving John a lengthy, and quite boring, overview of Cardiff's history. John just kept nodding his head as Paul droned on. It was clear that Paul wanted to show off his in-depth knowledge of Cardiff Technologies to John in front of the group. It was also clear that Paul wanted to take the opportunity to gloat a bit about what he thought was the obvious superiority of the R&D department in the Cardiff organizational hierarchy. Paul had quickly moved on from the -1 strain topic, focusing on the various gripes and concerns he had with the company, especially with his direct management. Others at the table had joined the conversation at this point as it transitioned from Cardiff's history, to pay scales, pay raises (or lack there of), family issues, husband and wife complaints, to finally the *really* important stuff like who was rumored to be sleeping with who at work.

John had not paid much attention to the -1 variant strain information at first. Those first few days and weeks on the job he had still been feeling out the workplace politics, trying to understand who was who in the Cardiff Technologies employee and management pecking order. He made it a point to just try to make friends with everyone, figuring it would give him the best shot at keeping his job. It wasn't until a few days later when it occurred to John that this mysterious -1 strain might be the answer to all his financial problems. Exactly when the original thought came to him he couldn't remember…it just seemed to materialize in his head overnight. His subconscious was hard at work while he slept trying to solve his financial problems. That's when he started to formulate the plan to steal the -1, which meant he'd have to start paying more attention to his new work pal Paul Travers.

Over the next few weeks he wove his questions for Paul into the lunchtime table chatter, picking up key pieces of information about the -1 strain and where it was kept on the Cardiff campus. Paul liked having an *in* with John and took pride knowing John was interested in his work, so it didn't take much prodding on John's part to get Paul to tell him everything he knew about the -1. The single key piece of information divulged by Paul concerned the R&D lab relocation planned in three weeks time. As it turned out, Cardiff planned to move the entire lab to make room for the new, and highly successful, XR9-2 production line. Cardiff wanted to complete the move quickly to cash in on the higher than expected commercial demand for the –2 treatment. John immediately recognized this upcoming relocation as his opportunity to make a play for the -1 strain.

It was almost as if this plan that had popped into his head was meant to be, synchronicity was what he thought it was called. His friendship with Tom leading to the job at Cardiff Technologies, which led to him meeting Paul, which led him to learning about the -1 strain, and now the lab relocation plan. However you looked at it, the universe seemed to be placing clear signposts for him to go down this path.

There was only *one* problem…and it was actually a big one. He had never stolen anything in his life, not even a candy bar. He remembers some of his childhood friend's five-finger discounting their way out of the downtown Five and Dime store, but not him. It wasn't that he never thought about it as a kid, he had. What kept him honest was his dad, and what would happen if he ever caught John even thinking about such things. If such a discovery would have happened to coincide with a night of his dad's drinking, John wasn't sure even God could have saved him.

But desperate times called for desperate measures and John felt his current financial situation qualified as desperate times. The lingering question for him in back of his mind was what to do with it once he stole it. He wasn't even sure what *it* was! Was it a formula written down on piece of paper? Maybe it was a beaker of some glowing chemical, steaming like a Halloween cauldron filled with dry ice. He had been trying to get more detailed information about the -1 from Paul, what it was and where it was, but could sense Paul's reluctance. John felt he was nearing the line of asking too many questions. He definitely didn't want to raise any red flags with Paul and have him report their conversations up to his management. Whatever *it* was, John guessed that it would be worth some money - quite a bit he hoped when he found the right buyer. He would figure all of that out later, first things first…how to get his hands on it.

The next weeks passed by in a flash, and John still didn't have a solid plan in place on how he was going to get his hands on the -1. In the evenings after work, he would pencil out all sorts of intricate plans. Plans that relied on precise timing of various lab technician's comings and goings, restricted lab entrance door's openings and closings, and so on and so on until his head ached each night before bed. None of it felt right. In the end he was out of time and knew he would just have to figure it out on the fly during the lab relocation. What was strange though was that he didn't feel panicked - he maintained that sense of synchronicity that everything would work out ok.

As relocation week neared John made sure to stay in close contact with Paul, listening intently for any last minute company change of plans or any new window of opportunity. When the official move started as scheduled the next Monday morning, John watched closely as the moving trucks began to shuttle the initial loads from the R&D building. Tuesday, Wednesday, and Thursday passed by, and still no plan epiphanies had come to John. He knew time was running out. So on that Friday morning John decided to take his morning break across the Cardiff campus in the R&D building's break room, which was down the hall from the lab where Paul worked. The R&D building was less than a 10-minute walk for John across the plant's central green zone area where many of the employees often took their breaks or ate their lunches relaxing on the lawn.

After making his way across campus that Friday morning, John entered the R&D building's break room only to find it empty. Like all the Cardiff break rooms, it was furnished with half a dozen or so tables for the employees to use during their 30-minute morning and afternoon breaks. The room also had four snack and two soda vending machines as well as a large refrigerator where employees could store their lunches brought from home. John quickly bought a bag of Lay's barbecue potato chips and a soda from the vending machines, and then picked a seat at a table that provided him the best view of the hallway leading up to the lab's restricted entry door. As John sat intently watching the lab door, other employees started to filter into the break room, buying snacks or retrieving their lunches from the refrigerator. He hoped no one would recognize him and start asking questions about why he was over on this side of the campus taking his break when his break room was no more than 20 feet from his workstation.

John waited patiently, his eyes glued to the lab entryway door, enjoying the Lay's chips and soda. He was just starting to think that maybe this whole -1 scheme wasn't going to work when he saw Paul coming down the hallway towards the lab entrance. He scooped up his chips and soda, throwing them in the garbage can as he quickly exited the break room.

Paul was now standing just outside the R&D lab's entrance door, he was preparing to swipe his security badge to enter. The R&D lab was one of the few areas in the facility that had restricted access with badge readers at every entry door. The regular Cardiff Technologies employee badges wouldn't work in the readers, you had to have a smart card badge with an encoded chip. The smart cards provided Cardiff security 24/7 tracking of all comings and goings of R&D lab personnel. John's badge was not encoded, he needed Paul to get him into the lab.

"Paul!" John shouted as he sprinted down the hallway from the break room towards the lab. Paul had swiped his badge and was now halfway through the lab entryway door. Hearing his name he stopped and poked his head back into the hallway to see who had called him.

"Hey - how's the big lab move going?" John huffed out as he approached.

"Oh...hi John." John could see the look of puzzlement on Paul's face, probably finding it strange to see John over by the lab. Recognizing the look of uncertainty, John knew he had to think quickly to avoid any awkward questions.

"Our damn break room vending machines are all out of barbeque chips so I thought I'd try yours...I was just heading back over when I saw you walk by." As he spoke, John made a mental sticky note to buy out any barbeque chips that might be in his break room's vending machine...just in case Paul got too smart for his own good and decided to check out his story.

"How's it going?" John wanted to keep the conversation going while he figured out what his next steps were to get into the lab.

The uncertainty and puzzlement slowly evaporated from Paul's face. "Just busy," Paul replied, "they're right in the middle of kicking us out of this building. I'll probably have to work this weekend to finish moving all my stuff."

John could see Paul wasn't too enthused about having to work the upcoming weekend - he saw the opening and took it.

"Could you use another pair of hands moving things? I don't have any plans and I'm *fairly* skilled at moving boxes." Paul laughed at this so John continued on quickly. "You just tell me what to move and where to move it," John said. He could see a bit of relief in Paul's eyes, maybe Paul saw some of the weekend becoming his again. After a very brief moment to think about it, Paul made the choice John had hoped for.

"Hey…you know what…that would be great, thanks!" Paul replied. His mood visibly improved by John's offer of help.

John then listened to another 15 minutes of Paul talking about his displeasure with how the company had mismanaged the move. Paul was not on board with the typical company-speak bullshit about being a team and expecting everyone to do "whatever it took" to get the move completed by the following Monday, even if it meant interfering with their weekend. Paul also repeatedly pointed out that he didn't expect to see any of the Cardiff bigwigs donating *their* weekend to help with the move. Throughout the rant, John continually voiced his wholehearted agreement with Paul's assessment - he wanted to keep Paul fired up and focused on John as the savior for helping out. After patiently listening to a few more minutes of complaining from Paul, they agreed to meet back that evening after end of shift to start moving his lab equipment.

"Who knows," Paul said, "if we get enough done tonight we might be able to watch some Sunday NFL games!" Paul's mood continued to improve as he thought about John helping out in the lab. He even invited John over to watch the Sunday football games at his place already assuming it would all work out. John politely said he would think about it...but knew he would not be going.

CHAPTER 40

Time seemed to slow for John that Friday afternoon. He watched the digital clock at this workstation slowly tick by the minutes, counting down towards the end of shift. All he could think about was getting into the lab that evening with Paul. He fought back the voices in his head telling him that he'd never find the -1...that his plan would fail. He just kept reminding himself that he'd found a way into the lab and he would find the -1. Just take one step at a time.

John met Paul at the lab entry door as soon as shift ended. Paul continued on about his plans for the upcoming weekend as he scanned his badge to open the door for the both of them. John lost track of how many times Paul thanked him for helping him out, he just kept responding with "Yeahs" and "No problems," not really listening to most of what Paul was talking about. Once inside the lab, John had a singular focus - locating where it, the mysterious XR9-1 strain, was stored in the laboratory.

The lab area was in complete disarray. The Cardiff facilities team had already started removing the desks and storage racks, and it looked as though they hadn't taken much care keeping things organized. Nothing was locked up and there were boxes, files, and all sorts of laboratory equipment piled on top of one another. It was obvious that the move wasn't very well organized or thought out, pretty much in line with what Paul had been complaining about all week around the lunch table.

John quickly surveyed the layout noting there were a number of interior rooms marked with "Restricted Access" signs on their now wide open doors. A few of the signs lay on the floor, haphazardly torn from the doors by the moving crews probably shoving the large office desks through the narrow door openings. John made his way into the room closest to him, volunteering to organize and box up the loose files that had been piled onto the desks and chairs. Paul shouted his agreement from across the room, none the wiser.

While Paul talked on and on in the other room about his favorite NFL team, the Cincinnati Bengals as John found out, and their chances of making the playoffs, John worked his way around the first room out of Paul's sight. Cabinet-by-cabinet, desk-by-desk, drawer-by-drawer, he searched the room making sure he boxed up paperwork and a few lab supplies along the way for show. He did the same for the second and third rooms. As he moved on to the fourth room, he checked in again with Paul to see how he was coming along out in the main room.

"Great," he said, thanking John for the hundredth time for helping out. From the looks of things, it appeared that Paul was almost done packing up his desk area...so John knew he had to quicken the pace of his search, time was running out.

Upon entering the next room John immediately noticed that it was still well organized, unlike the prior three that looked like a tornado had blown through. Another interesting thing about this room was that one wall was lined with very large gunship-gray colored cabinets. There were five in total, each one stood about six feet wide by eight feet high and had two large steel doors. John moved to the first cabinet and slowly opened the large doors, hopeful of what he might find inside. As he cracked the door and peered inside the cabinet his heart sank, it was completely empty - whatever was stored inside had been already moved. He proceeded to search the second, third, and fourth cabinets with similar results. Moving to the last cabinet, he made a quick visual check on Paul to make sure he was still busy, and then opened the cabinet doors. Inside were four black briefcases.

John had to catch himself from letting out a yell when he saw the cases. Looking them over, he saw each was affixed with an engraved bar code with the lettering XR9-1. John guessed this might be the official designation for the -1 variant strain Paul had talked about. Adjacent to each barcode there was other typed information, what he guessed might be the batch number and the date of manufacture. John quickly opened each briefcase in between keeping a watchful eye out for Paul in the adjoining room. The first three briefcases each held 10 small shiny silver metallic boxes. They reminded John of expensive looking sunglass cases, each was approximately three-by-six inches in size and secured in their own individual foam cutout within the briefcase. The fourth briefcase was only partially full, John counted seven boxes - the remaining three foam slots were empty. John picked up the last box in the row and opened it. Inside was a single glass vile nestled in a black foam shell...the vile was filled with some sort of liquid, this had to be what he was looking for. John quickly closed the metallic box and slipped it into his front jean pocket, un-tucking his shirt and pulling it down over his jeans to conceal the top of the box. He closed the briefcase and placed it back inside the cabinet, hoping no one would notice one less box. John was just closing the cabinet door as he spied Paul over his shoulder walking up to the room's entryway door.

"All ok in here," he asked.

"Yeah...yeah...just finishing up," John replied, his back to Paul as he latched the cabinet door handle.

"I'm done," Paul said, "how about we call it a night?"

"Sounds like a good idea to me, enough fun for one night," John joked as he turned around to face Paul, his hand smoothing out the front of his shirt over his jeans.

Paul thanked him once more for pitching in, and told him he would call him Sunday about getting back together to watch the NFL games.

After exiting the lab, they talked for a few more minutes in the Cardiff parking lot before Paul finally drove off. John watched his car exit the parking lot and turn onto FM240, his taillights fading into the distance. He then walked back and bought the remaining six bags of Lay's barbecue potato chips from his break room vending machine. The chips tasted great for dinner and no one ever did notice the one missing shiny silver metallic box.

CHAPTER 41

She was a beauty - Ham couldn't take his eyes off her. The *she* in question was a 26-foot Bayliner bass fishing boat with twin 225-horsepower outboard engines. She came with a Blue Starlight custom paint package and Bayliner's upgraded XLT limited edition interior, which included the 300-watt Bose stereo system. The system had 15 speakers, including composite tweeters and a new fangled sub-woofer design that could just about bounce you out of the boat if you turned it up past six on the volume dial. He told himself having that kind of stereo system in a *fishing* boat didn't make that much sense, but what the hell, he wanted all the bells and whistles for once.

Ham had gone along with John and Mary J buying the Harley's, but this boat, *this* beauty right here was what he wanted most of all. He'd always dreamed of owning a top of the line fishing boat like those he saw in the Field & Stream or American Angler magazine ads, but never thought he'd have the means to acquire one until the Cardiff payout. She was now within his reach.

He stood next to the boat in the salesroom, running his hand over the perfectly smooth glossy hull. Ham smiled as he surveyed the sales floor. The salesman he'd been working with all morning emerged from the back office area. As he strolled back over, Ham looked at the nametag pinned to his button down shirt. It read "Josh Peterson – At Your Ser   ," a smiley face sticker covered the last few letters. Josh had been gone the past 20 or so minutes, just out of view in the back office area, supposedly discussing Ham's last counter offer with his boss… the yet to be seen Sales Manager. The usual dance was being played out whenever you buy a car, boat, or RV. Josh reported back that his boss thought his last offer was "Outrageous!" and "They would be out of business in a week selling boats at that kind of price!"

As he stood listening to Josh's report, Ham wondered to himself if Josh was just in back having a cup of bad coffee and maybe a donut left over from the morning. Maybe catching up on the afternoon soap operas, and the all-powerful Sales Manager was just a façade. Stalling to see if he could outlast Ham.

Hoping eventually Ham would just give in because he wanted the boat. Betting Ham had just about anywhere better to be than a boat showroom for the entire day and just settle on the last price point.

The smile broadened across Ham's face. Little did poor Josh know that Ham was *truly* enjoying himself. He had dreamed of buying this boat since he was 12 years old following his first fishing outing on his uncle's Bayliner. Dragging out the negotiation and purchase process was only prolonging his overall enjoyment of the entire experience.

He had planned out this day for quite some time. That morning he'd made himself a full eggs, bacon, toast, and coffee breakfast. He wanted to make sure he didn't start getting hungry right in the middle of the negotiations. He had also brought along a couple snack bars and a large bottle of water. Ham wasn't going to be drawn in by the sale's office free coffee and donuts offer, no caffeine or sugar jitters for him to take him off his game. He was prepared and in this negotiation for the long haul.

Ham recognized that for once in his life he was in the sweet position of having the clear upper hand. He had the money, the time, and there were two local boat dealerships to play against each other. It was a simple supply and demand equation...and from the look in Josh's eyes, he thought Josh also understood the math. He positively intended to buy the boat today, even at the last price quoted by Josh, but he was just enjoying himself too *damn* much to stop and give in just yet.

Josh's voice came back into focus, "My boss says we just can't go that low." Ham could just start to hear the first hint of desperation in his voice. Ham knew he had him on the ropes, Josh was visibly tiring of the battle. "How about we throw in a three year extended service contract?" Josh offered up. No question about it this time, Ham definitely made out the plea of "Please just say yes" implied at the end of Josh's question.

They'd been at this dance for almost five hours. It was time for Ham to move in for the kill.

"I tell you what Josh, how about I meet you and your boss halfway on the price, *and* you go ahead and throw in that extended service contract...but let's go ahead and make it for *five* years."

Josh let out an audible sigh, it came out like a slow leak in a bicycle tire, as he turned to take this latest demand back to his boss. He looked like a beaten man.

"Let's go ahead and make that a best and final offer! I'd really rather not have to go looking across town at The Boatsman!" Ham called after him as Josh walked towards the back room. He threw in the local competitor's name to seal the deal. When Josh heard the competition's name mentioned he paused in his tracks, his shoulders visibly drooped as he restarted his walk back towards the manager's room. The smile on Ham's face had spread from cheek-to-cheek.

Ham was sure his offer would be begrudgingly accepted, with all sorts of "We're losing money on this deal!" declarations from Josh. He knew this because there weren't too many customers strolling in off the Danville downtown streets ready to drop $50,000 cash on a bass fishing boat. Supply and demand.

Josh came back even quicker than Ham expected, his hand already outstretched in a handshake. "We have a deal Mr. Hammond!" Josh shouted out. He sounded truly relieved to be done with this sale.

Ham ran his hand back over the sparkling Blue Starlight painted hull of his new boat as he shook Josh's hand.

It was exactly two months later that Ham decided to run for Mildred's town treasurer seat after he had found out about the LLF licenses.

CHAPTER 42

"Hit me again," John motioned to the barkeeper that he was ready for a refill. The bartender, a woman in her mid-60s, looked up from behind the bar where she had been busy putting away the freshly washed beer mugs and drink glasses.

"Time for another one?" she responded part question and part statement. She dried her hands on her apron as she grabbed the Jack Daniels bottle from behind the bar. The apron was emblazoned with the Third Base "Last Stop Before Home" slogan. She was a haggard looking woman, worn down from all the years tending the bottles.

"Tough day huh - I haven't seen you in here in a while…thought maybe you'd given it up," she took position in front of John, Jack Daniels bottle in one hand and the Coke auto-dispenser in the other. He sat watching her refill his drink glass, pouring the JD and spraying the Coke from the dispenser in perfectly mixed quantities. He had always been a little intrigued by the hand held spray system that all the bars had transitioned to over the years. The spray guns hooked up to some invisible, under the bar, behind the bar, in the back, system of tanks filled with Coke, Sprite and a variety of other sodas. At least that's how he envisioned it; it may have been a simple multi-gallon tank under the bar for all he knew. Just another one of the weird things you think about after a few JD & Cokes.

The barkeep's name was Wilma Blankenship. Her cracked and faded nametag just read "Wil ", the "ma" long since worn off on one side. John had always wondered if there was a story behind the missing "ma" or if it had just worn off over the many years of putting it on and taking it off. Wilma was the owner of the Third Base, but being bar's owner had not been her idea.

John had listened to her life story during one of the evenings he'd spent in the bar. Her husband had bought the place back in the '70s. He had always wanted to own a bar, her not so much but along for the ride. When he promptly died of a heart attack two years later, the bar was left to her. She learned after his death that he had dumped their life savings into the bar with the original purchase and fixer-upper costs. So it had been decision time for Wilma, either keep and run the bar or sell it and take a financial bath. So here she was 20 years later working the counter and listening to sad sorry stories told to her by the likes of customers such as John.

Watching Wilma, John assumed her current position in life probably wasn't what she had imagined for herself at her age. Pretty much the same feeling he had as he sat watching her pour the fourth drink. She was pouring it heavy in bartender speak, meaning stronger alcohol-wise than the normal mix. He gave her a sly smile to show his appreciation, catching her eye after she'd finished the pour and re-racked the bottle.

The bar had been mostly empty when John had first arrived, but was now filling up with the Saturday night drinking and party crowd. He eyed a group of chatty 20ish-year old guys who had congregated at one of the larger tables at the far end of the bar, but still within earshot. They were laughing and talking sports teams, drink preferences, and the latest status of an affair one of them had gotten involved in at work that had now gone south. Served him right John thought.

They talked and joked like they didn't have a care in the world, a far stretch from his current position in life. He was envious of their carefree mood. He could feel the alcohol starting to work its dark magic, and he found himself hoping, no wishing, the affair would lead to the man's divorce. Someone else should be going through some serious crap in their lives along with him, it only seemed fair.

Fair.

As soon as he thought the word it froze and stuck out in his mind, like bold oversized font on a printed page. It was one of those words that instantly brought back a flood of memories for John. He could still hear his prince of a dad's voice saying the word clear as day so many years after his death. He could also still see him sitting in his worn, food and drink stained, La-Z-Boy chair after a full night of drinking.

John remembers once where he or his mom had casually used the word "fair" regarding something that had happened during the day, just making small talk around the dinner table. Upon hearing the word, his dad had sprung on them like an African lion on wounded prey. "Fair is where they sell fuck'n cotton candy and candied apples! Life ain't fair – get used to it!" he was almost spitting the words out by the time he had finished the sentence. Life had not been fair to his dad and his dad had always held a grudge.

Yes…listening to group's mindless chatter definitely made him jealous. It made him angry with himself, with them, with the whole goddamned world all at the same time.

He felt trapped…trapped and desperate.

He threw back the last of the JD & Coke left in the glass tumbler and then sat holding it watching the last remaining drops of the drink slide back down the sides. He had to take the vile back.

John's original plan was to sell the vile of XR9-1. Well…*plan* may have been too strong of a word. How or to whom he could sell it to he had not figured out, but he guessed it had to be worth a good bit of money. Some serious money, enough money to make him whole, enough to bring him back to even with his mortgage, his bills…his life.

Even.

Even wouldn't have sounded that good a year ago, the word wouldn't have entered his mind. At that time he was riding a streak of gambling luck, a true lightning bolt that in his mind was never-ending. But now…how things change in life. Now…*Even*…sounded wonderful, peaceful, something so far out of his reach that it was almost painful to think about or even say the word.

He just needed a life reset. A re-do, a start over, whatever you wanted to fucking call it. He just knew he needed it. People did it all the time, you always heard about it on TV or read about it in one of the grocery story tabloids, why not him.

He was hoping the one single vile would give him his chance, *his* start over, *his* reset. How and to whom he ended up selling it to would work itself out he told himself.

But it was the *why* that kept eating at him, gnawing at his thoughts. Why would anyone want to buy such a substance? He told himself over and over to not think about the why...it wasn't his business. But it was one thing to tell yourself that, quite another to make yourself believe it. When he felt himself drifting towards the why question, he quickly told himself to mind the business at hand, what happened later or who ended up purchasing the vile would sort itself out. It was just a business transaction, that's all.

But the gnawing continued in the far reaches of his mind.

Something deep inside him, innate to his being, was fighting against his life fix-it plan. And it was telling him to take the vile back. Every time he pushed the *why* thoughts down and into the basement of his consciousness, they came crawling back up the stairs, knocking on the door to get out of the basement. He could swear he almost heard whispering sometimes in his ear, "Take it back...take it back...take it back."

John had been twirling the tumbler in his hand the past 15 minutes, thinking about the *why* and watching those last few drops lap around the bottom of the glass. He paused and slammed the glass down on the bar, trying to stop the damn whispers. He desperately wanted another drink but his head was already buzzed and fuzzy. What shreds that were still left of his better judgment were telling him he'd already had enough, probably too much already. It was the alcohol playing tricks on his mind...causing the whispers...that's all it was he told himself.

He slid the empty glass across the bar face. The glass came to rest against the backstop, that small edge trim that bar owners install to keep their glasses from sliding off of...or more often than not...being *intentionally* slid off of, the bar by drunk customers.

"I'm all done Wilma," he said out loud.

Wilma, who was tending to customers seated at the other end of the bar, did not hear John through the bar noise. She was busy pouring the other customer's drinks, making her stops along the way with the other patrons as she worked her way back to his end of the bar.

John threw down a $20 bill on the bar, enough to cover his last round and leave a nice tip for the old lady. He pulled on his jacket and headed toward the exit. The bar was now almost completely filled. He snaked his way through and around the groups standing by the bar and at the nearby tables. The white noise mix of bar patron laughter and chatter intermingled with the bar's TVs showing various sporting events filled his ears and made him feel dizzy. John paused for a moment, catching his breath and refocusing on the exit door. He suddenly needed to get out of the bar and into the cool night air. Taking a few more deep breaths, he told himself he'd feel better once he was outside. He pushed on through the remaining bar crowd and out the font door, a curtain of cool air striking his face as he exited the bar.

He stood just outside on the doorstep, letting the door behind him swing shut, cutting off the noise from the bar. He drank in the cool fresh night air, letting it wash over him. Washing away the smell from the bar's smoky interior and clearing his head of the cacophony of noises. He gazed up at the dark night sky, the rain had stopped and the clouds cleared, the evening stars now shined bright. He couldn't see nearly as many as he used to when he was a kid because of the Danville urban sprawl and city lights. He tried to remember the constellation names through the alcohol-induced fog. He took in a few more nice slow deep breaths, his mood continuing to improve since leaving the confines of the bar.

John slowly walked back to his truck, the parking lot now full with a few cars queued up waiting for spots to open. As soon as he was back inside his truck he quickly reached under the seat to check on the metallic box. Laying it on his lap, he took another look at the box's shiny exterior imprinted with the bright red biohazard symbol. He flipped the box over, the bottom had a white sticky tag attached to it labeled with: XR9-1, Lot Serial Number 1301.

John opened the box again to recheck the vile. There it sat…safely nestled in its black laser cut foam shell. He had half expected, mostly *wished*, it to be missing, which would have been a relief. But there it was, just as it should be, safe and sound.

John removed the vile from the foam shell and gently rolled it between his index finger and thumb. He held it up to the Third Base parking lot lights shining in through the truck's windshield, trying to get a better view of what was inside. The substance was a very dark brown color, almost black, and it *moved* like a liquid as he pivoted the vile from end to end. He did this a few more times, rotating it very slowly and watching it move, until he finally convinced himself that it wasn't a liquid…it just moved like a liquid. The powder, or whatever it was, looked to be made up of very fine particles, almost like sand but even smaller in size. It didn't *look* that deadly. A panicked thought flashed through John's mind…what if whatever was in the vile was worthless, maybe it had a shelf life that had long since been exceeded and it was just a vile filled with sand or powder.

John reinserted the vile back into its foam nest and placed the open metallic box on the passenger side seat. His eyes remained fixed on the dark substance inside the vile.

I have to take it back he thought. "I have to take it back," this time he said it out loud. "I have to take it back!" he repeated it louder this time, trying to make it stick. He repeated it another five times, each time a little louder, each time with a little more force until he was almost shouting it at himself as he sat alone inside the truck's cab.

Before he could talk himself out of it once again, he started the F-250 and steered it towards the Third Base parking lot exit, the shiny metallic box still sitting open on the bench seat beside him. As he drove he tapped through the pre-set radio station keys on the truck's dashboard, searching for some music to match his mood. He actually felt good, better than he had in a long time, and it wasn't just because of the alcohol. He smiled to himself as he hit the last pre-set radio channel key and heard Mick Jagger halfway through "Sympathy for the Devil". He turned up the volume and started singing along with Mick as he accelerated back onto the entrance ramp to the 425. John headed west this time, back towards Cardiff Technologies.

Saturday night traffic was light heading back into town. He pressed the F-250's gas pedal down and the truck quickly accelerated to 75 miles per hour as he merged into the fast lane traffic. The four miles back on the 425 went by quickly, and Mick was just finishing up as he exited the freeway. John made a right off the freeway exit onto FM240, the two-lane road that ran by the Cardiff plant.

He was still singing to himself after the song had ended and been replaced by a Credence Clearwater Revival song. Not being a big fan of CCR, John reached over to adjust the radio to find something with more of a rock beat...some more Stones would be perfect he thought. John noticed his mood was continuing to improve as he neared Cardiff, seeming to validate his decision to return the box. He glanced over to check the box on the seat beside him, he could barely make out the vile's shape in the dark foam shell. The street lights lining FM240 intermittently reflected off the vile's glass surface as he passed under them.

The high-pitched wail of a car horn brought John's attention quickly back to the road.

Just not quickly enough.

CHAPTER 43

Ham and Mary J sat silent in the Chili's parking lot…stunned.

"What the hell just happened?" Ham finally whispered.

"I just wish we would have known," sighed Mary J, "maybe we could have helped. Also…I don't think we should mention us for awhile…maybe give him a week or two…sound ok?"

"Yeah – I know I didn't feel right saying anything tonight and I could tell by looking at you at dinner that you didn't either. I'm going to call him tomorrow and see if he wants to come over and watch the Monday night Bengals game," said Ham.

"What about calling him tonight to see if he wants to join you for fishing tomorrow?" asked Mary J.

"I don't know...I think I should give him a day before I call. I'm guessing he might feel weird if I call him tonight after baring his soul to us at dinner. He looked embarrassed by the time he'd finished...I think 24 hours to let it settle in is best for all of us." Ham rubbed his forehead as he thought about how the night had turned out.

A light rain was just beginning to fall as Ham started the car. "I'm ready to get home...I hope this rain lets up for fishing" he said.

As he backed up, Ham glanced in his rearview mirror and saw John standing at the far end of the parking lot. He was standing alone right in the middle of the lot looking up at the night sky...the rain falling on him. The image only reinforced Ham's thought of giving John some time before calling him back.

They drove the rest of the way home in silence, thinking about the dinner conversation...thinking about John. They arrived home around 8 p.m. and Ham immediately went to work hitching up the boat and gathering his gear for the lake. It felt good to be doing something to get his mind off what had happened at dinner.

Mary J grabbed her umbrella from inside the house. "I'm going to walk down to the market and get some rocky road ice cream...a little walk in the rain will do me good to clear my head."

"Do you want me to come along?" Ham asked, even though Mary J knew he really didn't *want* to go...she knew he was just saying that to be a good husband. He really just wanted to get packed up and on his way to the lake.

"I'm a big girl," replied Mary J, "just get to the lake, I'll be fine."

They shared a quick kiss before Mary J walked out the front door saying "Have fun – catch us some dinner for tomorrow night!"

Ham watched her as she walked off in the rain, and then finished packing the fishing gear into the boat. He left the house for Lake Skinner around 8:30 p.m. His plan was to catch a few hours of sleep in the truck and get on the lake right at dawn - he pictured himself casting in that first lure just as the sun was rising.

As Ham drove west out of Danville he reflected on the night's events...thankful for the life he had...thankful for Mary J.

CHAPTER 44

John Tyler's brain synapses fired in double time, in step with his spiked heart rate being fed by an instantaneous surge of adrenaline released from his adrenal gland. During that brief moment when he'd glimpsed at the box on the passenger side seat, the F-250 had drifted across the double yellow line separating the FM240's oncoming traffic. When John looked up he was understandably confused at what he first saw and heard – the headlights directly in front of him along with the road line markings didn't add up and the blaring car horn filled his ears. His brain tried its best to catch up, processing the visual and auditory inputs as he came to the realization that his truck was now straddling the FM240's centerline. The double yellow stripe was now perfectly splitting the O and R of the FORD emblem attached to the F-250's front grill.

The oncoming car, what looked to John to be maybe a Toyota Camry, was already sliding off to its right hand shoulder in an attempt to avoid the much larger truck heading its way.

Dennis May stared in horror as the full size pickup truck crossed the double yellow line and barreled directly towards them.

"Watch out!" screamed his wife Cindy from the front passenger's seat...those would turn out to be her last words ever spoken.

They had just left Lucille's minutes before, having finally had the chance for a family dinner out to celebrate Dennis's re-election to his second term as Danville mayor. Dennis fought to maintain control of the Camry as he steered it onto the right hand berm of FM240, he could feel the car's tires begin to dig into the gravel and grass as it left the pavement.

The F-250 hit the Toyota at a slight angle from head on. The crash scene investigators would later precisely determine that the Toyota Camry, John had been correct with his split-second identification, impacted the truck at a 17.5-degree angle based on the car's skid marks and debris field. They also correctly surmised that the slight angle from center was due to the driver of the Camry making a last second attempt to steer the vehicle out of the path of the oncoming truck.

The F-250's engine bolts broke loose upon impact, sending the 600-pound V8 engine block through the truck's front grill and into the Camry's engine compartment. On its way, it gathered up and carried with it the driver's side front wheel, tire, and quarter panel. The sheet metal quarter panel was pushed into the car's front seat, slicing Dennis in two.

Immediately following the driver's side impact, the Camry pirouetted about the front passenger side tire and then became airborne. Once free of the ground, the car began to rotate almost perfectly around the car's forward to aft centerline. Once…twice…three times it barrel rolled through the air, before coming down on its three remaining good wheels - all three tires simultaneously exploding.

The car then skidded off the road riding on its rims - a shower of sparks shooting out from beneath the car's chassis. It finally came to rest, wedging itself up against the FM240's dirt berm. Coolant and fuel sprayed from under the engine compartment's tented hood. Severed engine hoses flew around like Medusas' snakes, knocking and banging about on the underside of what was left of the Camry's hood.

The Camry's radio was still functionally intact, playing Laura Branigan's "Gloria" through its few remaining working speakers. The music filled the now still again night air, even though all three of the car's passengers had ceased to listen. Dennis's wife Cindy along with their daughter Katie sitting in the back had been killed during the barrel rolls - their heads impacting the car's side windows on roll two and three respectively. Harvey, the family dog, riding in the Camry's back seat along with Katie, was ejected from the car on barrel roll three like a rag doll.

The F-250 faired slightly better.

John did not have time to alter the path of the F-250 prior to the collision. The truck's center of mass was directly on the FM240's double yellow line at impact. The truck's rear tires momentarily left the ground as it completed a perfect nosedive into the Camry's driver's side quarter panel, the truck's engine block being sent forward like a deadly projectile. After sending forth the engine block to kill Danville's newly elected mayor, the truck plopped back down onto the blacktop and continued on in a straight path down the road. Almost seeming to brush off the smaller car without notice.

The F-250's steering wheel airbag auto-deployed upon impact. John's head, which was bent forward from the initial collision and nose-dive of the truck, was directly in front of the steering column when the airbag was released. His head took the brunt of the airbag's force, and was driven backwards snapping his spinal column between the third and fourth vertebras. One final image was recorded by John's brain from his right eye's peripheral vision...that of the empty shiny metal box floating through the air above the passenger side seat. The glass vile had come free and was floating an inch or so above its laser cut foam safety shell.

John was dead by the time the glass vile hit the F-250's front windshield. It disintegrated upon impact, showering the inside of the truck cabin with fine glass splinters. The XR9-1's fine liquid-like dark brown particulates released from its glass confines like a puff of smoke.

If the F-250 had remained intact that day, most feel the biological contaminate would have been contained. Either within the truck's cabin or at least in a manageable area around the truck depending upon how the vehicle eventually came to rest.

But it didn't.

After impact, the F-250 slowly drifted to the right side of FM240, no longer under the control of a living John Tyler. The truck was still traveling at close to 40 miles per hour as it left the blacktop, running on through the scrub brush and small saplings lining the side of the road. The F-250 left a perfectly mowed path behind it, shearing off the small trees a few inches above the ground. The truck continued deeper into the tree line and came to a final violent stop as it hit a large oak, exploding into a fireball. The expanding fireball, fed by the F-250's recently topped off 48 gallon fuel tank, stood out stark against the moonless night sky...momentarily lighting the grisly accident scene as if it was high noon.

While some of the XR9-1 particulates were destroyed in the ensuing blaze, the majority rode the cloud of hot expanding air from the fireball. Expelled high into the night sky, they caught the stronger than normal easterly winds blowing towards and over central Danville.

Once again the Devil was chuckling...while God *must* have been napping that Saturday evening.

CONVERGENCE

CHAPTER 45

The first responders to the crash scene were from the Danville Fire Department's westside station. The city had two main stations, Danville's original fire station located downtown and the westside station built after the completion of the 425 freeway expansion.

The Danville fire department team consisted of 25 full time and eight part time firefighters. The 25 full time firefighters completed semiannual rotations between both stations to provide cross-training opportunities between the sites, while the eight part timers were equally divided and permanently placed at one or the other station. The department's captain was Bud Neely, a 27-year veteran with the department and a second-generation Danville firefighter. His father Ted had captained the Danville team that fought the '51 fire.

Bud was at the wheel of the lead fire engine number 113 with three of his team on board. The newest emergency squad from the town's emergency response fleet was following directly behind Bud's engine with two EMTs and one paramedic. Both vehicles arrived on scene approximately 17 minutes after the dispatch call came through from Danville's downtown 911 call center. Bud took great pride in his team's preparedness and response times, maybe not as fast as say a Columbus or Cincinnati first responder team but not bad for little old Danville.

The 911 phone call had been placed by a motorist traveling a few minutes behind the Camry on FM240. The caller, an elderly woman as reported by the 911 call center operator, was nearly hysterical as she described the accident scene. The woman had just kept repeating, "It's awful...it's awful..." over and over again. The operator, following the scripted call center protocol, kept her talking on the phone trying to gather as much information as possible for the first responder team.

During those 17 minutes the XR9-1 particulate cloud had dispersed in concentration and expanded in area, it now covered almost one square mile. The cloud was invisible in the night sky, fanning out in a semicircle from the initial impact point at the oak tree

- the cloud was being guided and shaped by the steady winds blowing out of the west. If it had been visible it would have appeared to be moving like a living entity...expanding and contracting, almost pulsating as the wind pushed the cloud directly east over Danville.

Upon arriving on scene, Bud immediately knew something was...*off*.

It wasn't the burning wreckages of the F-250 truck or what looked to be a mangled Toyota sitting a little ways down the road. Those he assumed would both contain one or more deceased occupants based on the 911 call center information and a quick visual assessment of both vehicles. That and Bud's 27 years worth of experience working accident scenes.

No, *off* was that there was no sign of the 911 caller. This was highly unusual since standard 911 call center protocol instructs the caller to stay on scene until the emergency personnel arrive. Of course it was not unheard of for the callers to disappear, not wanting any further limelight or attention from the soon to be arriving authorities and press. Adding to the missing 911 caller mystery was that there was a *third* car on the scene; the dispatch call center had only reported two. Mistakes were sometimes made, but this third vehicle looked to have an elderly woman draped over the open driver's side door. The scene just didn't add up…and he didn't like it.

Bud was still wrestling to make sense of the scene as he opened the driver's side door of engine number 113 and proceeded to step out. As he drew in his first breath of outside air, Bud's throat and chest immediately felt as if they had been set afire. His vision blurred…it felt like a swarm of wasps had laid siege to his eyes with hundreds of intense stings.

CONVERGENCE

CHAPTER 46

Upon the first glimmers of a path towards a commercially viable XR9-2 cancer cure treatment, the Cardiff Technologies senior management redirected the Cardiff research and development team away from any further investigation into the failed XR9-1 primate trials. An immediate Stop Work Order was issued and the investigation closed prior to finding the true root cause of the failed trials. What the investigation *had* shown prior to the plug being pulled was that out of the 20 primates subjected to the -1 strain, all 20 had died a clearly painful and horrible death.

The Cardiff scientist's electronic journals and handwritten notes from the XR9-1 investigation summarized the results as follows: KR of 20/20 for primate test specimens subjected to GPR of 1:1M.

When translated into layman's terms, this meant that there had been a Kill Ratio of 20/20 for the primate subjects exposed to a Gas Particulate Ratio of 1 part XR9-1 per 1-million concentration. The preliminary conclusion and recommendation by the Cardiff Technologies scientific team was short and succinct – "Extremely lethal, no commercially viable revenue streams identified. Recommend pursuing for possible military and/or weapon applications."

But no further investigations or live specimen trials were ever completed on the XR9-1 strain due to the overwhelming commercial success following the –2 variant trials.

None until *now…*

CHAPTER 47

Bud Neely's resting heart rate had been measured as a matter of course during his last yearly physical. The nurse had been so surprised when she took the reading that she actually ran the test twice. "Hmm...47 it is, that's *really* good Mr. Neely," she had told him during the checkup. She'd expected him to be closer to the normal 60-100 beats per minute resting heart rate for a 52-year old man. "Whatever you're doing just keep it up," she said at the end of the physical, "I wish all my patients were in your condition."

As Bud exited fire engine 113's cab that Saturday evening his heart rate was closer to 120 beats per minute. It wasn't because he had let himself go over the past few months, the spike in his heart rate was being driven by the release of adrenaline into his bloodstream. Bud's fight-or-flight instincts kicking into high gear in preparation for what lay ahead at the crash scene. Even after 27 years on the job, he couldn't fight his hard-wired human instincts. Bud could feel his heart beating fast and heavy in his chest as his senses became hyperaware of his surroundings. Firefighters and police officers often refer to this feeling as the *rush*. It was a term that contradicted the word's Merriam-Webster dictionary definition since time actually seems to slow as your senses kick into high gear, assessing and reassessing their surroundings.

As a result of his increased cardiovascular state, Bud quickly inhaled the XR9-1 particulates into his well-conditioned lungs. On its way to his lungs, the XR9-1 attacked the mucus lining of his throat and nose prompting the feeling that he had just swallowed liquid fire.

In parallel, the XR9-1 attacked Bud's eyes. He instinctively clamped them shut trying to ease the intense stinging…but it was too late. As he blinked once, then twice, he noticed his now blurred vision begin to darken around the outskirts. By his third blink the world had gone black - he was blind.

The Danville fire department owned biological containment gear, full Level-A pathogen biohazard suits and masks. But the gear sat unused in the department lockers at the westside station while the XR9-1 continued its attack on Bud Neely. From the information gathered on the 911 call, the dispatcher had no reason to believe this particular crash scene was anything but the run of the mill traffic accident.

Upon the XR9-1 reaching Bud's lungs, it set to work destroying the lung bronchioles, then seeped into his bloodstream by way of his pulmonary vein and artery. His immune system valiantly attempted to stage a fight against the invaders, but his white blood cells were quickly and efficiently eradicated.

Bud stumbled forward, one hand clutched to his chest trying to dig out the fire that had erupted in his throat and lungs. He reached out with his right hand to steady himself, blindly flailing to grab the driver's side door. He missed and collapsed to the ground, his eyes open but not seeing. He lay writhing on the ground for another 30 seconds before his heart finally succumbed and stopped beating. Death completed its job quickly, exactly 3 minutes and 37 seconds after Bud Neely had exited fire engine number 113. The total time elapsed from when John's truck impacted the oak tree and Bud's last heartbeat had been just over 20 minutes.

The remainder of engine 113's team as well as the supporting EMTs and paramedic suffered similar fates. Quick, painful, and efficient deaths – none of the team had time to react to seeing Bud collapse to the ground...and one by one they joined him.

Engine 113 and the emergency squad sat idling, their red and blue lights silently flashing and reflecting off the woods lining FM240. The night air was filled with the crackling noises coming from the burning wreckages of the F-250 and Camry. The large oak against which the F-250 had come to rest was now fully engulfed in flames, the fire now slowly spreading deeper into the woods. Every once in a while there would be a loud pop, as one of the burning vehicle's engine compartment fuel or coolant line expanded and eventually burst, tearing through the braided rubber.

On any other night the nearby tree line would have displayed a light show of sparkling firefly flashes...there were none tonight. On any other night the woods would have been alive with a symphony of cricket chirps...it was silent tonight.

Seven additional bodies had been added to the crash scene. The bodies of the four firefighters along with the three from the emergency squad laid strewn on the ground, none more than three feet from the doors they had exited minutes before.

The only sound of life came from the fire engine's cab radio as the Danville 911 call center dispatcher kept repeating his request for a status update from the scene.

CONVERGENCE

"Engine 113 please respond...engine 113 please respond...Captain Bud Neely *please* respond..."

CHAPTER 48

Ham sat in the truck as if in a trance, not moving - just barely breathing, listening to the radio. The sun had still not broken the horizon that Sunday morning. He had woke up not more than 30 minutes ago and had immediately switched on the radio, hoping to find some good music to launch the boat to...instead he heard KDAN's news reporter Jan Stevenson.

Jan was in a near panic. It was difficult at first for Ham to understand what she was talking about since she was almost shouting over the radio. Her voice was shaky as she tried to report out on the wave of information coming in from the first incident calls.

Unbelievable...surreal...no single word could quite capture the moment as Ham listened to Jan struggle to make sense of it all. He sat there stunned, listening to the frantic reports coming in to her and she trying her best to maintain a professional reporting demeanor. There were numerous reports of unexplained deaths coming in from all over the western portion of Danville. Jan was doing her damnedest to remain calm, telling people to evacuate the area if they were anywhere on the west side of the city. "Just get the hell out of there!" she yelled out over the radio. She also kept repeating what sounded like an officially prepared statement - instructing citizens to shelter in place and stay out of the area so that emergency personnel could enter to determine the exact cause of the emergency and treat the injured. She reported that the Center of Disease Control in Atlanta had been contacted and support teams were in route, they were expected to arrive in Danville within the hour. Jan also reported that an emergency response headquarters meant to house the CDC personnel was being set up just south of downtown.

Ham sat transfixed in his front seat, listening for hours to the chaotic reports coming through on the radio. His stomach sank as he thought about Mary J, his family, and John back in town. He felt helpless.

He tried repeatedly to reach Mary J on her cell phone, but each time the phone would ring twice on the other end and then go silent. The silence on the other end was the worst. Was she ok and it was just a case of the cell lines being overloaded by panicked calls between loved ones and friends? Or was she lying dead on the floor in their house, her cell phone buzzing by her outstretched hand. He told himself to not think the latter, but he couldn't shake the image.

"Damn it!" he shouted, trying once again to reach her only to hear the phone go silent again on the other end. He threw the phone onto the passenger side floor of the truck and pounded the steering wheel, feeling the first waves of panic come over him. Thoughts of driving back into town to find her bounced around in his head. The left rational side of his brain still winning out telling him "That's a *baaaad* idea." But the rational side was quickly losing ground as the minutes ticked by on the truck's radio clock.

He gathered up the phone and dialed John's number this time. The line didn't even ring like it had for Mary J…there was just open air on the other end.

He spent the rest of the day hunched over the steering wheel listening to the radio reports and re-dialing Mary J, John, and other family and friends in between. He finally got in touch with his mom and dad around 3 p.m. They lived on the far north side of town, and had stayed inside as instructed by the emergency broadcasts. His mom told him they "Felt just fine." She didn't understand what all the fuss was about, since looking outside her window all looked to be right as rain with the world. Ham just told her over and over to stay put and keep the windows and doors shut tight. He ended the call with an "I love you both," something he realized in the moment that he hadn't told them near enough in recent years.

At 8:30 p.m. that Sunday evening the National Emergency Broadcast System issued an all-clear radio broadcast. As Ham made his way back into Danville he felt as if he was living a nightmare, none of it seemed real. The town was almost deserted, he only passed three or four cars the entire way back...and there was a *strange* smell in the air. It smelled rotten, but not like rotten eggs, more like...death. He rolled up his windows trying not to think about it, he just told himself to keep driving, get home and find Mary J.

As he neared downtown, there were Ohio State Police and National Guard personnel positioned at every major intersection. Roadblocks had been set up and they were checking identification to make sure only residents passed through, trying their best to keep out the looky-loos and press that most likely were already descending on the town. The CDC had cordoned off all westside and downtown Danville neighborhoods...*their* neighborhood. Streets into and out of these areas were controlled and only CDC badged personnel were allowed access. The northern and southern areas of the city had been cleared by the CDC.

Inside these CDC controlled areas, fully suited contamination teams were still conducting door-to-door searches. Unbeknownst to the general public at the time, these searches were really just recovery efforts of the deceased.

As Sunday night wore on Ham still had not been able to contact Mary J or John.

CONVERGENCE

CHAPTER 49

The winds that Saturday evening pushed the blast cloud containing the XR9-1 particulates east from the FM240 accident site...east and directly towards downtown Danville.

At the time of the accident the Danville local weather reports indicated steady easterly wind speeds of 10-15 miles per hour, with intermittent gusts up to 25 miles per hour. A steady 10-15 mile per hour wind would have blown the XR9-1 particulate cloud across downtown Danville in just under 15 minutes. *If* there had been steady winds that night, the estimated loss of life would have been in the neighborhood of a couple hundred souls, worst-case maybe a thousand dead.

If.

The Center of Disease Control (CDC) analysts spent weeks after the event modeling the numerous weather variables that played a part in the aftermath. But a variable the CDC scientists didn't model, *couldn't* model, was that damn Devil chuckling and God napping *if* variable. That Saturday evening the Devil was probably standing just out of view...maybe just a few feet inside the FM240 tree line next to the accident site...smiling as he watched the fireball expand into the night sky.

That fall evening, due to an odd convergence of high and low-pressure systems merging together over Danville, the XR9-1 particulate cloud travelled quickly over the west side from the accident site and then stalled directly over central Danville. There it sat at an altitude of approximately 1100 feet for just over 12 hours. As the cloud stalled, the XR9-1 particulates began to gently...slowly...settle to the ground. A fine mist of the XR9–1 rained down on the good citizens of Danville that Saturday evening.

The post-event CDC computer simulation models matched remarkably well to the actual kill path taken by the XR9-1 cloud. The models, as well as real life, showed a kill zone emanating eastward across Danville from the accident site. The simulation model was color-coded, shaded from white to dark red to visually highlight areas not impacted or with low casualty counts (white and yellow), to those showing the greatest casualty counts (dark red). The mapping had a small yellow area at the accident site and then a large swath of dark red spreading outward, centered over downtown Danville. Here the XR9-1 concentration levels were on the order of 1000:1M - a *thousand* times the lethality levels originally tested by the Cardiff Technologies scientific team during the original failed primate trials.

As it turned out, Danville residents directly west of the accident site and XR9-1 release point, where Ham had been fishing that day, were completely unaffected since the winds carried the particulate cloud due east from the crash scene. Looking back afterwards, it was eerie to see the demarcation line of those affected versus those unaffected – life had been spared just a few feet west of the XR9-1 release point.

No clear, concise, evacuation orders were ever given to the Danville downtown residents that Saturday evening. This was due to a multitude of reasons. First off, the incident reports coming in to the Danville police and fire agencies were unclear as to *what* was causing these unexplained deaths, let alone any direction it may be heading. Secondly, the city lacked any sort of formal emergency response system to provide clear communication between the various emergency personnel that were trying to help. And lastly, and most importantly, due to the time of day the public and authorities had no way of knowing that they were dealing with an airborne particulate cloud. If the event had occurred mid-day there was speculation that the death count may have been much lower due to the *simple* fact that people would have, could have, seen the dark smudge of a cloud in the sky and been given at least some chance to evacuate outside its path. Instead most people either stayed put as instructed, directly in the cloud's path, or if they evacuated, some inadvertently actually went *towards* and into the cloud's path. This was confirmed post-event by the CDC's mapping of casualty positions versus places of known residence or where last seen.

The convergence stall eventually dissipated as the low-pressure system weakened and passed to the south, allowing the high-pressure system to regain its footing. The high-pressure system's easterly winds blew what remained of the particulate cloud along its normal eastward journey, across the Ohio state line and into Pennsylvania.

There were scattered reports of casualties as far east as New York City, but only 25 were ever directly linked to the event by the CDC. Many of the deaths reported outside of Ohio were compounded by non-related underlying health issues and removed from the event's final death toll. The casualty number officially recorded by the CDC in their final report was 25,314. The report, titled

"Danville, Ohio, XR9-1 Contaminate Release," also showed 99.9% of the casualties were within the Danville city limits.

Death was all-encompassing in the kill path of the XR9-1 particulate cloud. It had been indiscriminate in its killing, wiping clean all life forms it came in contact with. CDC response teams who entered the affected areas after the event reported back gruesome details - victims who had literally been struck down mid-step walking along city streets or eating at their dinner tables. Many asleep in their beds, their windows open to let in the cool night air...death had arrived unexpectedly.

CHAPTER 50

The next few days were a blur to Ham.

He ate little to nothing and when he did eventually force himself to close his eyes for a few minutes to rest, he would do so in his truck since he wasn't allowed back to their house...he felt dazed and barely alive.

His frantic search continued for Mary J and John, no one had seen either since late that Saturday night. John had not been seen since leaving the Third Base Tavern and the last verified contact with Mary J was just before 9 p.m., when she was seen leaving the market near their house after buying her rocky road ice cream.

The CDC and State Police were not much help either. Mary J was just one of many yet to be found. They were overwhelmed just trying to get their arms around the situation. Working to maintain a semblance of order and control and make sure the public didn't panic.

It was that Tuesday afternoon that the lists were posted around town. The lists held the names of the deceased as confirmed by the CDC and local law enforcement agencies. Word of who was or wasn't on the lists quickly spread around town, Ham stayed away from everyone not wanting to hear...not wanting to believe what he might see on the lists. He waited until that evening, Tuesday October 8th, when he finally drove over to the town library. The library had been designated one of the six posting locations for the lists around Danville.

It's strange what the human brain holds onto and what it chooses to forget. Some things in life you wish you would remember seem to get completely wiped clean from your memory banks, while others that you wish you could forget are burned into your memory forever.

Ham's crystal clear memories of that Tuesday made it feel as if it just happened yesterday.

The weather had turned sour that afternoon, with dark rain clouds moving in from the west. He still distinctly remembers the odd smell the rain brought with it as it began to fall. There was something *off* about it, it didn't smell fresh and clean, it didn't smell...*right*. Others obviously sensed it too - there were no children out playing in it as the drops fell that day. Mixed in with the smell of the rain was that of the wet fall leaves. The tall oaks surrounding the library had surrendered all but the last few. The rain quickly soaking the thick layer that covered the ground.

Ham remembers counting the library steps, a total of 37, as he climbed them to the front doors. He *even* remembers the shoes he was wearing, his favorite brown Red Wing boots.

A crowd had gathered at the top of the library stairs, with people clamoring to see the lists taped to the inside of the library's two front glass doors. A wide range of emotions emanated from the crowd and spilled out onto the library lawn. People were crying, some wailing, inconsolable after finding the name or names of loved ones on the lists. Others sat praying, some alone, some in large prayer circles on the library lawn. Still others were happy and laughing, dancing around crying tears of joy when they found their loved one's names not on the lists.

As Ham climbed the stairs, he took his place in line at the back of the crowd. He kept telling himself to stay calm, stay focused…just breathe. Ham could feel his heart rate quicken as he slowly advanced towards the library doors. He moved forward a few steps, now in sight of the posted lists. He was shocked to see that the number of sheets lining the door, there must have been 40 or 50 of them completely covering the inside of the glass. Each sheet was filled with a large number of names, the print so small you had to be right up next to the glass to really make out any detail. The line moved forward and Ham stepped into the front position against the glass. He started scanning the alphabetical listings, there were so many names it was a bit overwhelming. Ham's eyes jumped over the first few letter groupings down to the J section and then slowed to crawl down the names one by one.

His head swam and his legs went out from under him as he saw Mary J's name. Ham reached out, steadying himself on the man standing next to him.

"Ar...are you ok mister?"

Ham didn't immediately respond, he was trying his best not to fall to the ground. He closed his eyes, squeezing them tight to focus his concentration...away from the lists...away from the names swimming through his head.

"Mister...?" the man now had both his hands on Ham's shoulders, trying to steady him. "Are you sure you're ok? Do you need me to get you a doctor?"

"'I...I'm...I'm fine," Ham stammered reopening his eyes. "Thanks."

Ham took in a few deep breaths and then forced himself to return to the lists, re-reading Mary

J's name. The entire scene was dreamlike, he felt he could look down on himself from outside his body. He could see himself standing at the top of the library stairs in the crowd, the rain falling, that strange yellowish-brown dim lighting you get right before a big evening thunderstorm, the mix of emotions all around him.

Ham continued scanning down the names, passing by the R and S listings until he came to the start of the Ts. He reached out, and using his index finger started scrolling down the T listing, looking for and praying not to see John's name.

His was the last name in T section...John Tyler.

CHAPTER 51

A sharp knocking sound jolted Ham from his memories of that October day. He slowly turned his head towards the noise, blinking his eyes a few times, trying to remember where he was. He looked over to see a green and white park ranger's truck pulled alongside his truck. Lost in his thoughts he hadn't even heard him pull up. The park ranger was standing next to his truck – he tapped again on the glass with his knuckle, motioning for Ham to roll down the window.

Ham instinctively reached over and pushed down on the door console's electric window button. It took a moment for him to understand why the window didn't go down right away - the truck wasn't started so he had no power. He turned the key in the ignition and once more pushed the electric window button. This time the window did as commanded, and the glass lowered bringing him face to face with Ohio State Park Ranger Billy Sampson.

"I didn't recognize you Ham, it's been a while. Are you ok?" Billy asked as the window lowered.

It took Ham a few seconds to recognize Billy. They'd played on the Danville High varsity football team together their junior and senior years. While they'd been teammates they hadn't been that close of friends. Billy had played defensive end, Ham quarterback, so they'd spent most of their practice and playing time with their own offensive or defensive squads.

"Uh...yeah, I'm fine Billy, good to see you. I was just resting a bit before I go for a hike." His head was still a bit foggy from his trip down memory lane and he wasn't much in a talkative mood. What Ham was really thinking was that he'd like to end this conversation - quickly and without too many questions.

"You picked a great day for one. Hey - we should catch up sometime over a beer." Billy ended his statement with almost a question mark, hoping Ham would take him up on the suggestion.

"Yeah...yeah...that sounds good..." Ham's voice trailed off as his gaze returned forward out the truck's windshield, out towards the woods.

Billy took the hint. "Well...enjoy your hike Ham, good to see you again." Billy turned and headed back to his truck. He tipped his hat to Ham one last time before backing out of the parking lot.

Ham hit the up button on the door's console, closing the driver's side window. He sat back in the silence of the truck - the only sounds were that of his breathing and the dimming noise of Billy's pickup as he drove out of the parking area.

Looking out at the woods...thinking about it all.

It was hard to believe that almost 30 years had past since that Tuesday in October standing on the library steps. It felt like Mary J and John had just been there with him as he re-lived it again in his memory. Something he'd done a hundred, no, actually probably closer to a thousand times since that day...trying to make sense of it all...trying to find *meaning* in it all. He missed her *so* badly - he felt his chest begin to tighten up as he held back the tears.

It was several weeks after the accident before the full story was finally pieced together...it all leading back to John. Ham refused to believe it at first, but even he couldn't deny it as the evidence mounted of John's involvement with the XR9-1 release. Also damning were the results of John's autopsy, which showed his blood alcohol concentration level at .15%...far above the legal limit.

In those weeks and months following the accident, Ham had lost track how many times he heard people call John "an alcoholic," "a lousy drunk that ended up killing all those innocent people." At first he argued in John's defense, coming close to a few physical confrontations. But in the end...in the end, once he himself had seen the undeniable evidence against John, he stopped arguing.

Danville had slowly and painfully moved on over the years. Most newcomers to town didn't even know of the story. Ancient history, yesterday's news, in most people's minds these days. The story only somewhat interesting when it resurfaced each October in the town newspaper or on the local news, marking the anniversary and in remembrance of those that passed away.

Even Ham had been forced to eventually move on, the passing of time easing the pain but never fully erasing it...or the memories. He had been re-elected mayor that following fall and remained in the office for the next 21 years before finally stepping down. The town was sad to see him go, but he felt he had been at the reins long enough - it was time to give someone else a chance.

He turned back the key in the ignition shutting off the truck. Opening the door and stepping out of the cab, Ham took in his first breaths of the clean spring day air. The smell of fresh pine tree buds and wildflowers were in the breeze. He reached into the back of the truck bed and grabbed a small backpack. Swinging it over his shoulder, he closed the truck's door and started walking towards the trailhead sign at the far end of the parking lot. As he neared the signpost he stopped as he always did to read the bright yellow colored words engraved onto the sign's wooden faceplate. The first line read Johnson Tyler State, and on the second line below – Mary J's Trail.

The state park idea had been his very first action following his re-election to the mayor's office. It just seemed like the right thing to do, they both deserved it and they both would have liked it. He wanted to freeze in time the Neverland where they had spent their carefree high school days. Ham's idea obviously struck a chord with the citizens of Danville and the surrounding townships. A statewide initiative had been kicked off, with volunteers easily collecting the 10,000 names required to get it onto the following spring's ballot. It passed easily and the Ohio Parks and Recreation's trailhead team posted the new sign that October as part of the remembrance celebration.

No matter how many times Ham read the sign, it always brought a smile to his face. As he walked past he ran his hand over its weathered face, his hand pausing over Mary J's name.

They had been bulletproof, invincible, carefree kids wandering these woods. The realization of how fragile life could be not even crossing their minds. Not understanding that life can *sometimes* take a sharp turn for the worse in the blink of an eye...or in a slight change of the wind.

Ham walked on, a gentle knocking sound coming from the small backpack strapped to his shoulders. As he always did, he had brought along two beers for the hike. These days he rarely drank more than a few sips from one, but that didn't stop him from bringing them and giving John a toast. As he wandered deeper into the woods, he unzipped the side pocket of his jacket and reached in to grab a few of the candies he had brought along. Skittles - another one of the traditions for his twice weekly hikes.

He smiled as he walked, chewing on the candies, savoring the flavors. Who knows what he might find...what new discovery he might make in the woods today.

The End

EPILOGUE

The young boy stepped his way across the creek, dancing over the stone tops that sat just above the water's surface. He paused mid-crossing on one of the rocks, arms outstretched for balance – trying his best not to fall in, and called for Charlie to follow him. A large rambunctious yellow Labrador Retriever came galloping down the creek behind him, water dripping off the dog's thick coat.

The small creek he was walking fed into the larger Alum River 300 yards or so downstream. Flowing along with the creek minnows and crawfish, too small to be noticed by the human eye were very small particles. Particles very similar to the XR9-1 but *slightly* different...nature playing its part in the evolutionary dance over the last 30 years.

Alum River was one of six tributaries that fed Danville's Hoover Dam. It was there that these unseen particulates were settling at the deepest part of the dam, accumulating near the base of the wall where the dam locks were located. The concentration level was nowhere near that of the XR9-1 cloud that had rained down on Danville...but it was building...each minute of each day. The rivers continued to feed the reservoir, the dam locks continued to release water over its spillway, and the concentration level ever so slowly continued to increase at the furthest depths of the murky waters.

***

Stacy McClellan sat alone in the downtown Danville county planner's office. It was well past 7 p.m. on a Friday night, everyone else had left hours ago, eager to get home and start the weekend. He rubbed his temples as he reviewed the document laid out on the conference table in front of him, Danville's 20 Year Growth Plan. He was on the fence over the proposed plans set forth by the city council to either expand the city north, bulldozing a large swath of the northern woods near FM240, or go southeast towards Hoover Dam. He had been mulling this over in his head for the past three weeks, and today he had finally come to a decision.

Southeast it was. It would require draining a large portion of the dam, but it was nearing the end of its lifespan and scheduled for eventual

216

decommission - plans were already in place to bring online the newly built Jackson Dam. Stacy felt the flat valley floor would prove much easier to develop and be less costly to the city in the long run. Also, expanding southeast towards the more populous towns of Granville and Stevenson would provide additional economic growth opportunities to Danville and its citizens. It was a win-win in his mind.

Of course he had no way of knowing what was settling at the bottom of the reservoir as he signed off the planning proposal...

Maybe God was napping and the Devil was chuckling...once again.

About The Author

Scott Gulyas graduated from The Ohio State University in 1989 with a Bachelor of Science degree in Aeronautical and Astronautical Engineering. He completed his postgraduate study at California State University, Long Beach, obtaining a Master of Science degree in 2004. After working in the Aerospace industry for 23 years on projects such as the Space Shuttle and International Space Station, he began writing fictional novels – Convergence is his first published work. He currently lives with his family in California.